RACING WITH THE DEVIL

BRYAN SMITH

Grindhouse Press
PO BOX 540
Yellow Springs, Ohio 45387

Grindhouse Press #083
ISBN-13: 978-1-941918-96-8

In memory of people and times that have passed.

Other titles by Bryan Smith

ONE

October 31, 1987

EARLY EVENING TWILIGHT TIME ON a lonely stretch of winding two-lane road on the outskirts of a small town in Tennessee. The road is shrouded on both sides by tall trees that have mostly shed their leaves with the advent of fall. A blue jay sits perched on a lower branch of one tree, a silent observer of the tranquil peacefulness. The air is cool and a light breeze stirs the tips of thinner tree branches.

Then the blue jay turns and tilts its head.

Something is coming.

The discordant roar of some great beast. Beneath that roar is another unpleasant sound, an ominous accompaniment portending nothing good. The bird flaps its wings and flies away as the roar of the beast grows louder. By the time the red Camaro comes racing around the bend, it has already disappeared deeper into the woods.

The Camaro slews along the road, crossing all the way over the yellow lines dividing the lanes of faded asphalt. Inside the car, music blares, cranked to an ear-splitting volume. The band bursting through the overdriven speakers is Megadeth. *Peace Sells . . . But Who's Buying?* The car swerves and swerves again, repeatedly swerving back and forth across the yellow lines. Almost as loud as the music are the raised voices of the Camaro's four occupants. The heads of the guys in the back whip violently from side to side with the motion of the car. Long hair flies about like at a metal concert. A loosely held beer can comes free from a hand, trailing a spray of Budweiser as it bounces around the back of the car before dropping to the floor.

The guy who lost his grip on the can screeches in indignation.

That's alcohol abuse!

Sitting up front behind the wheel of the Camaro is Dennis Ayers, who is struggling mightily for control of the vehicle. Like everyone else in the vehicle in those moments, Dennis is screaming. Unlike his friends in the backseat, however, his screams are directed at a specific target.

Riding shotgun is Steve Wade.

They've known each other since they were little kids. A flash of memory cuts through the panic. Which is crazy. The danger here is real. It's getting darker by the minute and this road curves wildly. They could wipe out and go crashing into the woods any second now. But in that flashing instant the danger is overridden by a glimpse of the past. Dennis and Steve at ten years old, jumping up and down with tennis rackets gripped in their hands, manically playing air guitar as side one of *Double Platinum* by KISS spins on the turntable in the rec room of the Ayers' residence. Steve spins crazily about in an attempt to mimic an Ace Frehley guitar solo. He loses his footing and crashes into the stereo cabinet, knocking the needle out of the groove.

The whole time the little bastard is laughing madly.

Just as he's doing now between screams.

He's leaning over from the shotgun seat and has both hands locked on the steering wheel, jerking at it again and again and causing the Camaro to swerve dangerously each time. The guy thinks he's doing a funny thing, and being funny is a big part of his self-image.

He's the comedian of their group, an unpredictable wild card willing to do anything in the name of a laugh. This is far from his first life-imperiling stunt.

And right now the fate-tempting maniac is drunk off his ass, which always elevates his base-line level of crazy into something approaching a stratospheric range. So far Steve's antics haven't resulted in serious injury or harm to anyone, but luck like that can't last forever.

Enough already, Dennis thinks.

He takes one hand off the steering wheel and drills a fist into the side of Steve's head. The guy yelps in startled pain, but then he laughs again and somehow keeps one hand latched to the steering wheel. Dennis draws his fist back again and launches another punch at his friend. This one lands harder, knocking Steve sideways and finally forcing his hand to come loose of the steering wheel.

Dennis stomps on the brake pedal and the Camaro comes to a squealing halt in the middle of the road, straddling the yellow lines.

TWO

IN THE BACKSEAT, MIKE BURNETT'S body is pitched forward as the Camaro's tires shed rubber on asphalt. He's not wearing his seatbelt, which is unfortunate because being strapped in would've kept his face from smacking against the back of the shotgun seat's headrest. The law requiring the use of seatbelts only went into effect not quite a year and a half ago in Tennessee and a lot of times he still forgets to buckle up, especially when he's a passenger in someone else's vehicle. He's got this kneejerk thing against anything that reeks of the government telling him what to do, only now he's thinking maybe this was one area where those in authority possibly had the right idea after all.

He groans loudly as he falls back into his seat, then winces as he touches his nose to find out if it's broken. Doesn't seem like it, but it still stings from the impact with the headrest. Good thing it wasn't a brick wall he slammed into or it'd be broken for sure.

Belatedly, he realizes the headbanging music has ceased. Instead, he hears voices from the front seat raised in argument. Dennis is yelling at Steve, calling him crazy, calling him a stupid motherfucker. He threatens to drag Steve out of the Camaro and stomp his ass into the pavement if he doesn't calm down. Mike doubts anything of the sort will happen—it never has in the past—but Dennis has never sounded quite this pissed off before.

Mike sighs. "Dudes. Come on. A fight in the middle of the street is a dumb fucking idea. Good way to get us all carted off to jail if a cop comes along. And then we'll never find that party."

They don't hear him.

Still too busy yelling at each other.

Fuck it, he thinks. *Let them yell. Either they'll calm down or they won't. There's nothing I can do about it.*

A quick glance to his left confirms that Dave Robinson, his fellow backseat passenger, won't be aiding any effort to soothe tensions. His head is lolling to one side and Mike can hear him softly snoring behind his Spuds McKenzie mask. The mask is made of cheap plastic and each exhalation of breath makes the plastic vibrate. Wedged between his legs is a severely depleted gallon jug of PGA (pure grain alcohol) punch.

Now Mike looks at his empty right hand and again laments the loss of the nearly full can of beer that went flying thanks to the whipsawing motion of the car prior to its screeching halt.

A 12-pack carton of Bud cans is shoved up under the seat in front of him. He leans forward and extracts yet another one from the dwindling pack. He pops the tab as he sits up again, taking a big swig of the lukewarm brew. Mike isn't quite wasted yet, but at his current pace he'll get to that point before long. This doesn't bother him. Getting wasted is always the goal on these outings with his friends. Especially on a night like this one.

A special night.

He's treated Halloween with a nearly religious reverence since the days of his childhood, loving the costumes and the spooky spectacle of all the decorated houses in the neighborhood. No surprise for a kid raised on a steady diet of monster movies on the afternoon *Creature Feature* shows. Now he's too old for trick-or-treating, but that doesn't mean the spooky fun has to end. If anything, getting older only means being able to take the fun to an even crazier level.

Up front, Dennis and Steve are still yelling at each other, though it's not quite as heated as it was moments ago.

"You didn't have to hit me fucking twice, asshole. I mean, shit, you're the one driving. You could've stopped the car any goddamn time. And for the record, you caught me off-guard with those punches. I'd kick your ass in a fair fight."

The words are laced with angry defiance, but Mike doesn't need to see his face to hear the smile underneath the words. He gets the impression Steve is struggling not to burst out laughing.

"There you go again, making excuses for your shitty juvenile behavior," comes Dennis's equally defiant retort. "I'd knock you out in a minute, go all Iron Mike on your ass."

"What the fuck, man? Are you saying my ass makes you hard as iron? Look, dude, I'm an open-minded motherfucker, but I'm just not into buggery."

A brief silence follows this comment.

Mike tenses.

Then the guys up front both burst out laughing.

Mike lets out a sigh of relief and takes another swig of the lukewarm Bud. He's about to take yet another one when his ears belatedly begin to perceive a sound previously obscured by all the yelling. He twists around in his seat and takes a look out the back window. There's a car behind them, pulled up almost right to the Camaro's rear bumper. The car is blacker than the night itself and has tinted windows. If not for the moonlight glinting off the body of the car, it might be almost invisible in the darkness. The car kind of gives him the creeps.

Mike thinks it's a Z28, the slightly fancier version of a regular

Camaro. The one Dennis drives is an RS, with a few less extra features, maybe slightly less horsepower under the hood. In Mike's opinion, the distinction means exactly jack and shit. A real gearhead would almost certainly feel otherwise, but so what?

The Z is still just sitting back there, its engine idling. Which is weird because even though Dennis's car is currently stopped in the middle of the road, there's more than enough room for the Z to go around them. And why is it pulled up so fucking close? This whole situation is starting to feel genuinely ominous and for the moment everyone else is completely oblivious to it. Dave's still passed out and the guys up front are still laughing and exchanging increasingly ludicrous personal insults.

Mike clears his throat and raises his voice. "Uh, guys?"

Before anyone can respond, the Z backs up a few feet, swings into the next lane, and begins to pull forward. Mike experiences a short-lived moment of relief. The feeling dies an abrupt death as the Z pulls even with the RS and stops instead of speeding off into the night.

Mike gulps.

The beer can, slick with condensation, almost slips from his grasp.

He tightens his fingers against the wet aluminum and thinks, *Oh shit.*

THREE

DESPITE HIS WINDOW BEING UP, Dennis hears the throaty rumble of the Z28's engine as the car pulls up alongside his RS. Right up until the moment that sound intrudes, he's still laughing and shaking his head at the dumb but undeniably funny shit Steve is saying. The laughter fades as he turns his head and sees the other car.

Steve sees it too and snorts in a derisive way. "Check out Bruce Wayne over there. Looks like he got an upgrade on the fucking Batmobile."

Dennis grunts, but says nothing.

As always, his friend is trying to be funny, but this time it's hard to miss a distinct note of unease underneath the forced mirth.

Dennis frowns. "What does this fucker want?"

Mike pipes up from the backseat after clearing his throat. "I was trying to tell you guys. He was right up on our bumper until just a second ago. I'm getting some real bad vibes here."

Dennis nods, his frown deepening. "Yeah, me too. He's probably pissed about me being stopped in the road. Like I give a fuck. Motherfucker needs to get over it and move the fuck on."

He hits the button to lower his window and as soon as it's down he sticks out an arm and waves his hand in a "go on by" gesture. The only response from the hidden other driver is a loud revving of the Z's powerful engine.

This elicits another derisive snort from Steve. "Does that son of a bitch want to race? Out here in the boonies in the fucking dark?" He laughs nervously. "Shit. He's high as fuck. Or even crazier than I am."

Now there's a disturbing idea, Dennis thinks.

He makes the "go on by" gesture again, this time in a more emphatic way. His impatience is growing. He has no intention whatsoever of racing anyone on a two-lane back road distinguished by sharp curves. Even in daylight the chances of any such contest ending in anything other than a deadly crash are virtually nil. At night? It's a goddamn certainty.

As dusk deepens, the impenetrable blackness of those tinted windows exudes an implied malevolence. He fears there are darker intentions here beyond a highly dangerous race challenge. An impulse to simply hit the gas and speed away tempts him strongly. He's seized by the sudden conviction that getting away from the black Z28 as fast as possible might save their lives. His fingers flex and curl tighter around the steering wheel as he shifts in his seat. He's maybe one more breath away from taking his foot off the brake and jamming it down on the gas pedal when the Z's passenger-side window begins to slide downward. In that moment, his heart slams so hard in his chest he's surprised it's not audible to everyone around him.

With the lowering of the Z's passenger side window, he's at last able to discern the dark outlines of two figures occupying the other vehicle's front seats. Dennis twists again in his seat and leans toward his own open window, his mouth opening to say something, but before he can utter a single word, a slender, pale arm emerges from inside the Z. Grasped loosely in ivory fingers with dark-colored nails is an open beer bottle.

Dennis frowns.

What the fuck?

The slender hand flings the bottle at him. The shadowy assailant's aim is true and he's forced to duck in order to avoid being struck by the glass projectile. He does, however, get hit with a spray of warm beer before the bottle crashes instead against his dashboard. There are shouts of surprise and outrage from Steve and Mike, but these barely register to Dennis. He experiences a flickering instant of in-stinctive fear, but the feeling is almost immediately overtaken by a surge of explosive rage. Teeth clenched tight and frothing with fury, he jams his gear shifter over to park and begins to get out of the car.

He hears laughter from the occupants of the Z28 as his door be-gins to open, a sound followed by another revving of the Z's engine. Before Dennis can open the door wider and set even one foot on asphalt, the Z28 speeds away, its tires squealing and back end fishtail-ing a moment before getting on a straight course. A moment later, its taillights disappear around one of the road's many swooping curves.

His rage still simmering, Dennis stares through his windshield for a moment at the now empty open stretch of road ahead. Just letting them go is the smart move here. No one got hurt and the surest way of keeping it like that is to just let it fucking go. They can proceed with their night as planned and just chalk this up as a weird incident they can laugh about later. Things could take a really bad turn if he does anything else.

He *knows* that.

Not so deep down, he really fucking does.

But the level of alcohol in his blood and the potent anger still gripping him make for a volatile mixture. He's aware of his friends talking, saying things to him, but his mind processes none of it in a normal way. The voices are just noise. He sees his hands shaking on the steering wheel and knows there's only one way to purge the rage filling him like a toxic poison.

Payback. I gotta fucking get some.

He opens his door a little wider before pulling it shut again with a lot more force than necessary.

Then he shifts gears again and hits the gas.

FOUR

THE RELIEF MIKE FEELS AS the Z28 speeds away and disappears around the bend is so huge it temporarily sucks all the energy out of him. After leaning forward and peering through the gap between the front seats throughout the brief confrontation, he flops backward, heaves a sigh as he slouches down in the seat, and takes a long swallow of beer. Now that the moment of stupid drama has passed, they can again focus on the truly important things—getting fucked the fuck up and finding that epic Halloween party.

He turns his head to glance again at Dave Robinson.

Still out like a light and snoring harder now, making the cheap plastic mask vibrate more noisily than before. The sound is akin to someone lightly blowing into a kazoo. It's almost funny. Mike leans over and gives the guy a hard poke in the shoulder. The attempt to rouse him fails.

He's about to try again when Dennis closes his door and hits the gas.

Once again, he is whipped from one side to the other as the Camaro goes around that bend at high speed. Dave falls against him and Mike has to shove him away, fighting to push his still-unconscious friend down into the seat in a way he hopes will prevent him from being tossed around the back of the car like a fucking rag doll. The effort yields only slightly successful results, in part because Dennis seems determined to keep driving like a demented, demon-possessed Mario Andretti on crack. Dave's Spuds McKenzie mask hangs askew now and Mike can see a thin trickle of drool hanging from a corner of his mouth. The plastic jug between his legs has tipped forward and a stream of the high-octane PGA punch is pouring out of the open container to the floor. Mike makes a grab for it but misses as another sharp spin of the wheel sends him careening back to the other side of the car.

Up front, Steve is shouting at Dennis, urging him to slow down and stop acting so crazy. This reversal of their usual roles is so stark Mike momentarily feels as if he's slipped into some bizarro alternate universe, like on that one old episode of *Star Trek*. As he at last manages to sit up straight again, he is gripped by an apprehension nearly the equal of the immense relief he felt mere moments ago. Dennis hasn't stated his intentions here, but Mike can fucking guess. Any chance of him letting the incident slide died the moment that beer bottle came sailing into the Camaro. Mike's only hope at this point is that whatever happens next doesn't end with anyone seriously hurt or worse.

An instant later, he hears a violent hacking sound from the other side of the backseat, one so loud it startles him nearly out of his skin. Mike's head snaps to the left and he sees Dave struggling to sit up straight. He's awake now and from the sound of things his stomach is revolting against the toxic mixture of PGA punch, warm beer, and drive-thru burritos roiling around inside him. That terrible hacking sound is him trying hard to expel a tidal wave of vomit, a difficult proposition in his current position. He's also whimpering and Mike hears genuine terror in the sound. Dude is scared he's gonna choke on his own vomit and go out like a rock star, a not unreasonable fear given how far down Mike shoved him into the seat.

Mike groans and grimaces.

Aw, fuck.

The loudest hacking sound yet rips through the interior of the car like the sound of a gunshot. It's a horrible thing to hear, but it has the effect of silencing the screaming argument going on up front.

Steve twists around in his seat and pokes his head through the gap between the seats. "The fuck is happening back there?" His face registers only annoyance at first, but this quickly gives way to a wide-eyed look of alarm. "Holy fucking shit!"

The car slows some as Dennis pipes in. "What's going on?"

Steve glances at him. "Fucking Dave is choking to death, that's what the fuck is going on. Holy shit."

The upper part of Dave's torso lurches upward as a brackish brown fluid comes spilling out of the mouth hole of the Spuds McKenzie mask.

Mike tears the mask away, the thin rubber band encircling Dave's head yielding with an audible snap. The lower part of Dave's face is covered in more of that gross brown goop, which he supposes largely consists of burrito filling. He thinks the guy ate four of the goddamn things. At least. Dropping the mask, he leans over and grabs hold of Dave and works to get him closer to a fully upright position. All the while, Dave moans and whimpers with tears spilling from his eyes. Mike is assailed by guilt. His friend wouldn't be struggling so hard if he hadn't shoved him down like that. Okay, yeah, it's a thing he did in a desperate attempt to solve another problem, but the fact remains this is still partly on him, thus it's now also on him to keep the dumbfuck from choking.

Right after he finally gets Dave upright, there's a moment where Mike thinks things are gonna be fine, with no further drama or mess. Dave's face is flushed a bright shade of red and sheened in sweat, but he's breathing almost evenly and there's a calmness in his eyes that definitely wasn't there a moment ago. His eyelids flutter and he looks like he's on the verge of sliding back into la-la land.

Then his eyes and mouth open wide again and he leans abruptly forward as he makes another of those nerve-twisting hacking sounds. His throat looks grotesquely swollen for a moment, bulging from the girth of some escaping alien parasite, like something out of one of the cheap and gory horror movies they rent weekly from Smyrna Video. Mike expects to see the slimy, eyeless, teeth-gnashing head of the monstrous creature any second now, squirming and squealing as it emerges from Dave's mouth.

What happens instead is nearly as disgusting.

Dave makes one more strangled hacking sound and then a stream of brown vomit comes spewing out of his mouth like water blasting out of a fire hose. Some of the noxious stream of puke hits the back of the seat in front of him, but much more of it goes flying through the gap between seats as he turns his head, a good bit of it splashing against the gear shifter after Steve gets out of the way. There are cries of disgust from up front as the car starts swerving again. A second eruption of vomit paints the roof of the car as Dave flops backward.

He's still coughing and hacking as the Camaro comes to a squealing stop at the edge of the pavement. The projectile puking phase of his episode of sickness appears to have come to a merciful end, but he's still upchucking brown gunk. It's rolling out of his drooping mouth and sliding down his chin and now Mike thinks it looks like gravy being poured slowly out of a bowl.

The Camaro's doors pop open.

Dennis and Steve get out.

His own stomach churning from the powerful stench permeating the interior of the car, Mike pushes the seat in front of him forward and gets out, too.

FIVE

AFTER HAULING A STILL DAZED Dave out of the backseat, Dennis drags him over to the shoulder of the road where he can finish puking with less risk of getting run over by oncoming traffic. Right now the chances of that seem relatively low. Aside from the sounds of Dave being sick—and Steve's ongoing proclamations of revulsion—things are quiet out here in this patch of rural nowhere. He hears no other vehicles approaching but knows well how fast that can change. There's no shortage of locals who treat these old back roads like they're the redneck Autobahn, especially at night when they're loaded up on Black Label beer and cheap white trash drugs.

Dave hasn't quite stopped heaving, but the spasms are much weaker now and there's not much more than spittle coming out of his mouth. Dennis leaves him to it and goes back around to the other side of his car and leans in to put on his hazard lights. His face twists in disgust as the smell hits him and he quickly backs out again.

He opens the Camaro's hatch and finds some beach towels still in the trunk from when the four of them went to a water park during the summer. There's also some crushed beer cans and a nearly empty bottle of Popov vodka. One of the towels is emblazoned with the Budweiser logo. It belongs to Dave. Dennis grabs it. Holding his nose this time, he again leans into the car and uses it to soak up all the puke that hit the gear shifter. There's even some of that brown gunk on the radio and the air vents above it. He mops up every bit of it and is even able to wipe off the back of the driver's seat. By then the towel is pretty foul-looking. He carries it almost daintily by a corner as he traipses into the ditch by the shoulder of the road and drops it there.

Dave makes a sound of pitiful dismay. "My Bud towel."

Dennis grunts as he kicks some brush over the towel. "Sorry, but that thing is definitely a piece of toxic fucking waste now. I don't want that gross thing in my car. Also, consider this a lesson in knowing your limits."

Mike snickers. "Or maybe don't eat five hundred fucking burritos and guzzle a gallon of PGA right after."

Dave groans and wipes sweat from his forehead. "It was only five burritos, you exaggerating motherfucker." His voice is so slurred he hardly sounds like his normal self. He straightens slightly and starts patting his face as his still-flushed features register confusion. "Whoa. Hold on. Where's my Spuds mask?"

Mike chuckles. "Sorry, dude. Spuds is DOA."

Dave makes another sound of dismay. "Aw, man. I was gonna wear that at the party."

Dennis rolls his eyes at the mention of the party. He was as fired up about it as anyone, but not so much anymore. Now the whole night just feels tainted. He's convinced they should call off this quest to find the backwoods shindig and head back into town, where it probably won't be too difficult to find a smaller Halloween gathering. Just do what they always do and cruise up and down the main drag until they find someone who knows what's up. There's always some-one with the scoop on parties if you search long enough. It was how they found out about this supposed epic spook night throwdown in the boonies in the first place.

Also, as pissed as he is about the horrendous mess inside his car, this incident with Dave has at least allowed him time to cool down again. He felt angry enough to kill a few minutes ago, an idea he finds disturbing even in the midst of his beer buzz. In truth, he's not quite as buzzed as he was before, the rage seeming to have burned away some of the alcohol in his system.

Dennis steps up out of the ditch and stands at the side of the road with his friends. "Okay, fuck this. We've done enough searching around for this fucking party, going up and down side roads, driving around in fucking circles. We could waste the whole goddamn night looking for this thing. Let's just find something to do in town."

Mike scowls. "Are you kidding me? That party is supposed to be epic as fuck."

Dennis laughs. "Yeah, right. According to Darryl Frykowski. That fucking burnout has smoked more dope since junior high than Cheech and fucking Chong put together. The guy can barely tie his shoes without help and we're supposed to believe he has the inside track on the party of the decade? One we haven't heard a word about from anyone else, I might add." He makes a dismissive gesture and shakes his head. "Come on, man. Think about it."

Mike's scowl shifts, gradually becoming a dejected frown. "Well, shit, man, when you put it like that. *Fuck.* Maybe you're right. And I was looking forward to that thing so bad."

Steve claps a hand on his shoulder in a gesture of manly commiseration. "Me, too, bro. Me, too. It's a goddamn tragedy. We'll remember where we were and what we were doing when we experienced this moment of heartbreaking disappointment for the rest of our lives."

Mike grunts, nodding. "Like with our parents and the JFK assassination."

"Exactly, bud. Exactly."

Mike shakes his head. "I'm gonna beat Frykowski's ass next time I see him. The way he described it just sounded so goddamn cool. Hundreds of people partying on acres of open land. Dozens of kegs and a live band. No neighbors around for miles to get mad about the noise. Wet t-shirt contests and a mud-wrestling pit. Loads of horny college girls from Murfreesboro. Why would he make all that up?"

Dennis shrugs. "Who knows? Hell, maybe he believed it. I think Frykowski has a hard time telling fantasy from reality. Might've just been some bullshit he saw in a movie while he was stoned out of his fucking mind." His attention shifts to Dave, who's looking a little less woozy now. "What about you, man? Up to getting back on the road without being sick all over my car again?"

Dave's pained expression conveys a deep level of embarrassment. "Yeah, sorry about that, but I couldn't help it. I think I'll be okay now. I could use a beer to help settle my stomach."

Dennis looks at Mike. "We got any beer left?"

Mike nods. "A few cans of Bud. A stray bottle of Heineken for some reason. Don't know where that came from."

Dave laughs. "I shoplifted that from the SupeRX while you were buying the Bud. Fucking forgot about it." The laughter fades away as he looks down. "Hey, why are my pants all wet?"

Mike explains about the spilled PGA punch.

Dave groans. "Fuckin' A. What a goddamn waste."

Dennis grabs another beach towel from the trunk before slamming the hatch shut. "We'll do a beverage restock before heading back to town. Let's go find a gas station."

The four of them wearily pile back into the Camaro.

Before getting in, Dennis hands Dave the second beach towel, instructing him to soak up as much of the spilled punch as he can with it. Then he settles in behind the wheel again, puts the Camaro in gear, and roars off into the night.

SIX

THE DISAPPOINTMENT MIKE FEELS AT missing a party that probably only ever existed in the permanently fried brain of an inveterate stoner is real, but it isn't long before he realizes this development is probably for the best. Some of the big parties he's gone to with his friends these last few years have resulted in several of the most memorable experiences of his young life. A few of the bigger ones were crazy as hell and made him feel as if he was living out scenes from a movie, some new version of *Animal House* or *Fast Times at Ridgemont High*.

These are only fleeting moments in his life, however, such a miniscule amount of time compared to the much greater sweeping swathes of time spent alone in his room at his parents' house. Time that passes while his friends are out living the other parts of their lives that don't involve him. Going to work. Dating various girls. He tends to hold on tightly to those party memories in those alone times, clinging to them so fiercely they become almost hyper-real in his mind.

It's pathetic, really, how unfulfilled his life is in so many of the other, much more important areas. He knows it's past time to grow the fuck up and take responsibility for himself. Maybe even chill out on the drinking a little.

He's twenty-two now. Not a fucking kid anymore.

And yet he feels stuck, almost hopelessly so.

Pushing the depressing thoughts out of his head, he twists around in his seat. There's a double-sided tape case wedged up against the window in the space behind the backseat. Grabbing the case, he plops it down in the space between Dave and himself. The case is his. He brought it along for the evening, as per usual for these boozy outings with his friends.

He opens one side of the case and starts perusing the contents, which includes tapes by Motorhead, Motley Crue, KISS, Kix, Metallica, Anthrax, Judas Priest, Iron Maiden, Krokus, Black N' Blue, Hanoi Rocks, and so on. There are also a few punk tapes. Fear, Black Flag, and the Misfits. That's the headbanging and anarchy side of his portable music collection. If he opens the other side, he'll find tapes by R.E.M., Love and Rockets, The Replacements, The Smiths, and other staples of college rock radio. That side will remain closed for the evening. Just not right for the vibe.

His index finger slides over the tapes until stopping on one at the bottom of the middle row.

"Who's in the mood for some Guns N' fucking Roses?"

There are general noises of assent.

He takes out the *Appetite for Destruction* cassette and passes it up front. Steve takes it from his fingers, opens the case, and pops it in the tape player. The album came out just a few months ago, in the last week of July, and they all have their own copies they've listened to countless times by now. It's the one tape Mike makes sure to have with him wherever he goes. The music resonates with him in a way few things ever have. When Axl Rose sings about drinking and driving and fucking junkies in the gutter, he sounds like he means it, whereas a lot of bands with songs about the same things often sound like they're just striking a pose for the mall kids who buy their tapes.

This music sounds so much more authentic, rawer and stripped of pop fluff. It's badass street poetry. There's none of the gloss of bullshit bands like Poison or Bon Jovi. The video for the album's lead track, "Welcome to the Jungle," has been getting some decent play in the late-night hours on MTV, but Mike doubts the band will ever take off in a big way. They're obviously too down and dirty for mass public consumption.

As soon as those first notes of "Jungle" hit, Dennis reaches for the radio's volume knob and cranks it way to the right. Up front, Steve goes "Awww, yeah" and starts bouncing around in the shotgun seat again. Mike starts bobbing his head as the song really kicks in and he sees Dennis doing the same behind the wheel. Even Dave's perked up enough to start moving to the music, which blasts from the Camaro's speakers with bone-rattling intensity. Mike feels it engulfing him like a force of nature, sweeping him away to some higher state of rocked-out bliss. It's perfection, this feeling. This moment. He wishes it could last forever.

And the music has undeniably worked a form of magic, wiping away the disappointment of a few minutes ago and dispersing that dark cloud of introspective depression. Suddenly he feels invincible and badass again. He grabs one of the few remaining cans of Bud from the almost empty carton and chugs down half of it in one go.

The Camaro keeps gliding along the dark road as the last notes of "Jungle" fade away and "It's So Easy" begins. Mike is so lost in the music he hardly takes note of where they're going. It doesn't matter. Dennis knows his way around out here better than the rest of them, probably because they've always left drunk night driving chores up to him. He doesn't drink any less than the rest of them when they're out cruising around. The concept of a sober "designated driver" is something they still laugh at. It's just that, among the four of them, he is by far the best at maintaining control of a vehicle while under the influence. There's virtually no discernible difference between his drunk driving and his sober driving, at least as far as Mike's ever been able to tell.

Or maybe they're all guilty of a little willful self-deception on that count. It's certainly possible alcohol has rendered them all oblivious to any indicators of danger in the way Dennis handles the Camaro while intoxicated. There's also undoubtedly an element of tempting fate in this equation. They're young and have never had anything truly bad happen to them, and even though it's crazy to think this way, it sort of feels like that's how it's gonna stay forever and ever. Nothing can touch them. Death and tragedy are foreign concepts. On a perhaps subconscious level, driving fast down dark roads while under the sway of various intoxicants is a testing of the limits of a seemingly charmed existence, of seeing just how far they can go without hurtling all the way into the abyss.

As "It's So Easy" nears its conclusion, Dennis shifts gears and slows down. At first it isn't clear why and for a moment a dark thought penetrates Mike's improved mood. The black Z28 has reappeared and now it's blocking the way ahead. Dennis is about to stop the car and attempt yet another confrontation with the Z's driver. Mike leans forward and takes a squinting look out at the stretch of road visible through the windshield. The Camaro's high beams are on, but all he sees is empty gray asphalt. No sign of the Z. The car continues to decelerate and within another few seconds Dennis takes a right turn down a side road Mike didn't even glimpse until they were right up on it.

Mike leans back and braces himself as Dennis changes gears again and hits the gas. There's a slight downward slope to this new stretch of road and when Mike glances out the side window the shadowy terrain flashes by in a blur. This has the effect of making the car feel like it's going much faster than it actually is, not that they're going slow by any means. The Camaro's engine revs and they go even faster. Mike glances out at the shadowy scenery again and experiences a strange mixture of fear and exhilaration.

They could hit some unseen object in the road and wipe out, the Camaro flipping end over end as they go flying into the woods. A fallen tree or some sizable piece of roadkill, something they'd never see until too late. He tells himself that won't happen, no fucking way, because Dennis is in control and he knows what he's doing. He has the impossible luck of an ace World War II fighter pilot somehow successfully threading his way through wave after wave of Japanese Zeros, miraculously never getting hit by any of the high-velocity lead ripping through the smoke-filled air.

Mike drinks the rest of the beer and continues to stare out at the night.

It could happen, he thinks. *It really fucking could. One fucking deer carcass in the wrong spot could end us all.*

Dennis drives on for miles and miles, the Camaro tightly hugging the curves of this seemingly endless road. The tape keeps rolling in the cassette player. They hear "Nightrain" and "Out Ta Get Me." Axl's razorblade voice is like the devil himself talking to them, screaming, growling, urging them on toward whatever dark destiny fate has in store for them. The rest of the beer is drained. Then Dennis finally slows down again and takes another right turn into darkness. After that, it's off to the races yet again, the engine revving and revving. An abrupt shift in elevation as they go around yet another sharp curve results in the car's tires leaving the ground for a moment.

Mike gasps.

He feels his breath catch in his throat, his heart swelling like a balloon as he braces his feet against the floor again, for all the fucking good *that* will do.

This is it. This is it. Oh, shit.

Then the car's tires thump down on asphalt as the Camaro swerves over the yellow line into the opposite lane. The *wrong* lane. But their luck is in yet again. The road is still empty. Dennis quickly brings his car back into its proper lane, but maintains a high rate of speed, barely slowing at all. The close call does nothing to reawaken the part of him that errs on the side of caution, his normally predominant side. He's in full-on daredevil mode now. Maybe it's the music stirring something primal inside him. Maybe it's all the booze. Maybe it's the invigorating freedom of speed and all these empty fucking roads.

Probably it's all those things and more.

Just when Mike starts to think the high-speed ride through rural darkness might never end, Dennis again slows the Camaro and turns down another side road only he saw coming. By then side one of *Appetite* has ended and there's a few moments of strange silence until the tape clicks over to side two. This time the turn Dennis has taken is to the left, and to Mike's great surprise he catches a glimpse of bright artificial light somewhere a little up ahead on the right. The fluorescent sign of a convenience store is faintly visible through some trees, and in a few more moments the store itself comes into view.

Steve squelches the volume on the first haunting notes of "My Michelle" and shifts around in his seat in a way that indicates he popped off his seatbelt at some point while Dennis was blazing recklessly through the night. Probably not a stellar idea for anyone sitting up front as that was happening. Then Mike belatedly realizes he never strapped on his own belt. Didn't even think of it. Despite his continuing ambivalence over the new law, he finds this mildly alarming under the circumstances.

Oh, well. What's done is done.

Steve squirms as they near the store. "We stopping? Because I gotta piss like a Russian racehorse."

Dennis glances at him. "What does that even mean?"

Steve snorts. "Man, *I* don't fucking know. It's one of those weird things my grandad used to say all the time. Does a Russian racehorse piss more than racehorses from other fucking countries? Who the fuck knows? So are we? Stopping, I mean?"

Dennis says nothing.

He answers by turning in at the parking lot entrance and pulling up to the gas pump closest to the store. There are four pumps in total, but no vehicles are parked at any of the others. In fact, there's no sign of any other vehicles at all, which strikes Mike as slightly odd. There should be at least one other car somewhere, maybe parked out of the way in a corner of the lot, because how else would the clerk on duty get here? Unless maybe the clerk doesn't have a car and was dropped off at the start of his shift by someone else. Sure, it's possible, but he can't imagine anyone who'd want to risk getting stuck out here with no quick way home if something unexpected happened. Like if there was a robbery or the power went out.

Steve throws the passenger-side door open and leaps out of the Camaro the instant it comes to a full stop. He's in such an overwhelming hurry to relieve his painfully swollen bladder that he neglects to fully shut the door. The tail of his black trench coat flaps around as he runs full-tilt toward the store and leads with his shoulder as he bangs through one of the glass entrance doors.

Dennis laughs. "I've never seen that motherfucker move so fast. Maybe when we used to play football in your front yard, Mike, but definitely not since then."

Mike smirks. "Yeah, I think you're right. So are we getting more beer or what? Some gas, maybe?"

He starts to reach for his wallet.

Dennis turns around and glances at him through the gap between seats. "Put that away. I've got it. What do you want? Bud again? Maybe a six of Beck's? That's your favorite, right?"

Mike frowns. "You don't need to do that."

Dennis opens his door, but glances at him again before getting out. "Do me a favor and put five dollars of regular unleaded in my tank. I'll pay the clerk."

He gets out before Mike can say anything else.

Dave gets out with him and they head for the store.

Mike has mixed feelings about the unasked for act of charity. He has some money, but not a lot and Dennis knows this. Not that his low fundage situation is any big secret. He hasn't worked anywhere in months and is in no huge hurry to acquire gainful employment. It's a problem for sure, but he fears getting locked into some shitty job when what he really wants is to go back to school.

No.

That's not really true. Not exactly, anyway.

That's the lie he tells himself. The one he almost believes, if only because he repeats it so often to his worried parents. He doesn't know if *they* believe it, but there's no doubt they desperately hope for it.

What he *really* wants is to move to Los Angeles and somehow get into making movies. *Horror* movies preferably. But that seems like an impossible pipedream. His parents won't support that. They certainly won't help finance it in any way. Depression starts creeping in again as he thinks about all the things tethering him to his shithole hometown.

No money. Not nearly enough to get all the way across the country, at least. No connections of any kind out there in Hollywood, anyway, so if by some miracle he could actually make the journey, he'd end up living on the streets and sleeping in his car. He foresees not even the slimmest possibility of anything resembling a happy ending to that scenario.

I'm stuck. Fucking stuck. Probably forever.

He shakes the feeling off—or tries to, anyway—and gets out of the car.

SEVEN

THERE'S A LOT THAT'S STRANGE about this convenience store out in the middle of nowhere. For starters, it's a Union 76, and there haven't been any of those in this area since he was a kid. There was a 76 at the end of Wickman Road, three miles from the neighborhood where they all grew up, but it's been gone since before the end of the '70s. Dennis remembers using his allowance there on Big League Chew and packs of *Star Wars* trading cards. Other times he'd get a paperback adventure novel from the spinner rack next to the counter.

Of course, it's impossible not to notice the complete lack of other vehicles in the parking lot. His thinking on the subject closely mirrors what went through Mike Burnett's head upon taking note of this mere minutes ago, though he does wonder if the clerk's car might be parked somewhere out of sight. Behind the store, for instance. Didn't look like there was an area back there for parking, but he supposes this is at least minimally possible.

Then he goes into the store and there's no one behind the counter. He experiences a first flutter of foreboding. This is odd, but maybe there's a good explanation. The clerk could be in the storeroom in back, taking care of some work-related task or hiding out in there long enough to smoke a joint. One of the guys he used to work with at Winn-Dixie now works the overnight shift at a gas station closer to town and he does the same thing every night.

These are reasonable enough explanations and he's on the verge of letting the matter drop for the time being, but then a more morbid possibility floats up out of nowhere. Maybe the clerk *is* behind the counter and the reason he's not visible is because he's lying in a pool of blood on the floor, shot dead by some robber minutes before Dennis and his friends arrived. This deepens his unease for the simple reason that it's so horrifically plausible. Gas station robberies aren't exactly an unheard-of phenomenon. In some bigger cities it's almost an epidemic. People didn't start calling these places "Stop N' Robs" for no good reason. They're easy targets for junkie criminals looking to score some quick cash, especially the ones a little out of the way like this store.

Though it's the last thing he wants to do, he knows he needs to check behind that counter. Before doing it, however, he takes a moment to survey the store's interior and is struck by how eerily empty and quiet it is. The only other person inside the store—that he can see, at least—is Dave Robinson. Steve, presumably, has disappeared into the bathroom. Dave is staggering around in the snack aisle, the cardboard handle of a case of Budweiser dangling from one hand, a bag of pork rinds and a package of beef jerky clutched in his other hand. How he can still have an appetite after vomiting so profusely such a short while ago, Dennis does not know. He hears Dave mumbling something as he lurches around and it takes him a moment to decipher one small snippet: "*Loaded like a freight train. . .*"

Dennis can't help but chuckle.

Dude, you're loaded, all right, but from the look of things your train's about to derail.

He turns back toward the counter, takes one step in that direction, and once again stops cold in his tracks as yet another unbidden disturbing thought turns the blood in his veins to ice.

That fucking Z28.

The black car is still out there somewhere, roaring around in the night, driven by some belligerent thug looking to cause trouble. Maybe the people in the Z showed up here first. Maybe one of them shot and killed the clerk. It's another unsettlingly plausible scenario. He imagines taking a peek over the counter and seeing some poor fucking bastard with a bloody hole in his forehead staring blankly back at him. The conjured image is so vivid it triggers a twinge of queasiness, a sharp clenching of his stomach. An impulse to hurriedly roust his friends out of the store and leave now tempts him quite strongly, but in the end he decides against it.

He has to do the right thing here.

At this particular stage of his life, he is not the most responsible human being on the planet. He has no illusions on that count. However, he also strongly believes this is only temporary. He's existing in a reckless phase that will soon pass. At his core he is an essentially decent person who before long will settle down and be a regular suburban family guy, just like his father and grandfather before him.

And those are men who'd never dream of turning away from a difficult or even scary thing like this.

He swallows a lump in his throat, takes a deep breath, and approaches the counter. The fear is still there. His heart is pounding. But he's not going to stop or turn away this time. He arrives at the counter, takes one more big breath, and leans over it.

Oh, thank fuck.

The floor behind the counter is devoid of fresh corpses. There are no signs of hastily mopped-up blood. The relief he feels is huge, but now the mystery only deepens. They've been in the store for a few minutes now. The clerk has been absent long enough that he probably should've locked the store up before pulling a vanishing act. Anyone could walk in here and loot the place without much fear of being caught in the act.

Dennis backs away from the counter and cups his hands over his mouth. "*Hello!?*"

The elevated volume of his voice should be more than loud enough for anyone lurking in the storeroom to hear it. The shouted word is so loud, in fact, it startles Dave and sends him crashing into a large display of Funyuns at the end of the snack aisle. Dave loses his grip on the case of Bud cans and it hits the floor with a heavy thump. Some flailing about ensues, during which he sends numerous yellow bags tumbling to the floor. He eventually falls atop the bags, popping some of them open as he lands on his back.

Dennis groans and shakes his head.

Jesus fucking Christ.

He glances out at the parking lot, paranoid some bored cop will pick this most inopportune moment to show up and start hassling them. On his own, he's fully capable of playing it cool in a situation like that despite his level of inebriation, at least for a short time. Long enough, at least, to stay out of a cop's way and get out of the store without his drunkenness being detected. He's good at faking sobriety when necessary. For a while.

Dave's another story entirely.

He'd be an absolute disaster in the presence of a cop right now.

Fortunately, there's no cop car in the parking lot. His bright red Camaro is still the only vehicle in sight, but that can't remain the case forever, even out here in the sticks. Someone else will come along eventually. Maybe a cop, maybe someone else, some local yokel. Either way, they need to be gone from here before that can happen.

They need to pay for their shit and be on their way. *Now.*

Unfortunately, the missing clerk has unhelpfully not responded to his shouted inquiry.

A door opens somewhere near the rear of the store and for a

fleeting moment Dennis thinks it might finally be the clerk emerging from his hiding spot, but it's just Steve coming out of the bathroom. At the same time, Dave rolls over with a pained groan and starts trying to get to his feet.

There's a look of fearful confusion on his face as his gaze finds Dennis. "Jesus Christ, man, what's with the fucking screaming?"

Steve comes up the snack aisle, giving Dave as wide a berth as possible as he walks on by him. One of his Doc Martens stomps a yellow bag flat. "Yeah, dude, what's the ruckus about?"

Dennis rolls his eyes in exasperation and sweeps a hand toward the counter. "There's no clerk. I was trying to get the motherfucker's attention so we can pay and leave."

Steve's head cranes slowly around as he does a thorough scan of the store. Then he cocks an eyebrow as he looks at Dennis. "You haven't seen anybody this whole time? Because it feels like I was pissing for about an hour in there . . ."

Dennis shakes his head. "I'm starting to think we're really the only ones here, weird as that sounds."

Steve smirks. "Then I fail to see the problem. Free beer, man! Let's load up fast and burn fucking rubber."

Dennis scowls. "We're not criminals."

Steve's smirk deepens. "Dude, seriously? I'd probably need more than one hand to count all the laws we've broken already tonight." He turns slightly and jerks his head in Dave's direction. "That motherfucker has already shoplifted beer at least once today. You've been driving at excessive speeds with a blood-alcohol level I'd wager is way over the legal limit. Granted, we're not hardened felons, but we are far from innocent souls. And, shit, it's not our fault nobody's here. So let's grab some cases and go."

By this point Dave is finally back on his feet.

He retrieves the case of Bud he dropped and staggers closer. "I'm with Steve on this one."

Dennis laughs. "Of course you are."

The bell above the door rings and Mike comes into the store. "Done pumping the gas." His eyes flick about, taking in the mess made by Dave and the absence of anyone behind the counter. He also appears to sense he's interrupted a dispute of some kind. "So . . . what are you guys up to?"

Dennis grunts. "We're robbing the place, apparently."

Mike nods slowly. "Huh. Interesting." He takes another look around and heaves a breath. "So do I have time to take a leak before you do that? Because I've gotta go pretty fucking bad."

"Yeah, go ahead," Dennis tells him. "I've gotta check something else before we do this dumb fucking thing."

Mike heads off to the bathroom without another word.

There's a set of swinging double doors to the right of the counter area. The storeroom is almost certainly on the other side of them. He heads over there and slowly pushes through the doors, peeking around the edge of one as he checks out the dimly lit space. He sees stacks of boxes along the walls. He sees a dinky little metal desk covered with papers and a mop bucket sitting next to it. A small lamp on the desk provides the only illumination. What he doesn't see is anything resembling a person, but it's dark and he needs to be sure, so he steps fully into the storeroom and conducts a closer, much more thorough examination. In a corner there's an open door to an employees-only bathroom. It's small and dirty. There's no one in there, either. There's no one in here at all, other than himself. It's a confounding, irritating conclusion, albeit an undeniable one.

What the fuck is happening here?

There's another door in the middle of the back wall.

He goes to it and lightly grasps the silver doorknob, jerking his hand away when he feels how cold it is. The cold is at an almost freakish level. It's like gripping a ball of ice. He can think of no obvious or sensible explanation for this. This is a moderately cool evening in the fall, not a freezing day in the dead of winter. The room itself isn't cold at all. So what the fuck?

After hesitating a few moments, he reaches out and tentatively touches the doorknob again. This time he doesn't feel that shock of freezing cold. The metal feels normal in his hand, like it should. This is both puzzling and a little scary. It's some spook show shit. He's positive he didn't hallucinate that cold feeling. An impulse to turn and flee almost overpowers his lingering curiosity, but instead of doing that he tightens his grip on the knob and turns it.

The door comes open with a slight grating sound.

Through the opening he sees only the grassy hill behind the store and the line of trees that stands beyond it. He pokes his head through the opening and takes a fuller look around. Closer to the store and off to the left is a small barren patch of ground. There's a little table there with attached bench seats. It's cheap and rickety-looking. A picnic table for the destitute. There's a scattering of cigarette butts on the ground. He figures this must be where employees take their breaks, but there's no one out here.

An icy wind blows, making him shiver as goosebumps appear on his arms.

Fuck this.

He steps back into the storeroom and pulls the door shut with greater than necessary force. After backing off a few more steps, he swears he sees a rime of frost appear on the metal doorknob.

He shakes his head. "Uh-uh. Nope. Fuck it."

He's still far too drunk to even begin making sense of this. There's something wrong about this place. Something *weird*. Something impossible to fathom. All he knows for sure is he doesn't want to linger here even one second longer if he can help it.

He hurries out of the storeroom and sees that Dave and Steve have already departed. The idea of being alone in this strange building freaks him out and he wastes no time following his friends out to the parking lot.

EIGHT

THE BATHROOM IS DISGUSTING. IT'S a small space in-
tended for use by just one person at a time. Instead of multiple stalls
with doors, there's a lone toilet and it's clogged nearly to the point of
overflowing with sodden toilet paper and unflushed feces. The toilet
seat is down and drenched in what appears to be fresh urine. There's
more urine on the floor at the base of the toilet. A yellow puddle of
piss has pooled into the corner to the right of the toilet. The overall
aroma is decidedly not pleasant.

Mike grimaces as he walks over to the toilet, moving slowly and
taking care not to let the soles of his shoes slide on the wet floor tiles.
The last thing he wants is to take a tumble and end up rolling around
in piss. If that were to happen, he thinks he wouldn't be able to stand
it. He feels queasy just picturing it and knows he'd wind up puking
his guts out like Dave did earlier. The small space is so sickening he's
tempted to back out of it and go around to the back of the store to
relieve himself there. Wouldn't be his first time utilizing that option

after slamming a bunch of beers. Not any big deal in his opinion, especially if one takes care to do it out of easy sight of anyone else, but as he's recently learned, some people take a dim view of any form of public urination.

One night a few weeks back he and Dave took a leak out behind a Kwik Stop while Dennis waited in the Camaro. Steve wasn't there that night because he was too busy squabbling with his now ex-girl-friend. Upon their return to the parking lot, some big and bearded good ol' boys in overalls started shouting at them. They stood in the bed of a Ford pickup truck brandishing shotguns. First time in Mike's life anyone ever pointed a gun at him in anger. As it was happening, Mike was too surprised to feel fear. That came later, when he was sober the following day. Despite that lack of fear, however, he was stunned into inaction. Dave's reaction was virtually identical. He's not sure how bad things might have gotten if it'd taken Dennis much longer to notice what was going on.

Fortunately, however, he did finally notice, after spending those first few moments of the confrontation lost in the music blasting from the Camaro's speakers. After cutting the volume on Tesla's *Mechanical Resonance*, he popped out of the car with an inexplicably unconcerned grin and started playing peacemaker. Telling jokes and displaying impressive natural diplomacy skills. Before long, the giant, bearded Neanderthals were laughing with him. They were no longer pointing their shotguns at Mike and Dave, though it was clear they still weren't exactly happy with them. They finally let it go when Dennis handed over a six-pack of Bud tall boys as a peace gesture and coaxed half-hearted apologies from his bewildered pals.

Weeks later, Mike still can't believe it.

Labeled a pervert for taking a piss on a dumpster. It's not like he was flagrantly flapping his exposed dick around in public. Shit like that is yet another reason he hates his hometown. The fucking rednecks. Always looking to start shit with anyone different from them.

He doubts anything like that would happen here tonight. This place seems fucking deserted. He's confident he could duck out back and take care of business with virtually zero risk of a similar incident.

The problem is his need is too urgent. He's not at all sure he'd make it back there in time to avoid pissing his pants. Resigning himself to what he has to do, he edges even closer to the toilet, scrunching his face up as the stench emanating from it intensifies. Normally he wouldn't piss into a toilet with the seat down, but no way is he touching that disgusting goddamn thing. Nor will he attempt to lift it with the toe of a shoe. Given his level of intoxication, he'll end up rolling around in piss for sure if he tries anything like that.

At least he doesn't have to take a shit.

His stomach clenches just at the thought.

He unzips and takes out his dick, taking care to aim the strong urine stream that begins almost instantly at the center of the clogged toilet bowl. Sure, this place is already a fucking wreck, but he sees no reason to make it even worse. Unlike Steve, he's not a *total* barbarian. Some poor schmuck will have to clean this cesspool eventually.

Mike laughs softly as he tilts his head back and stares blearily at mildew-stained ceiling tiles.

At least I'm not you, he thinks, imagining this theoretical store clerk none of them have seen. *Whoever you are. This place is a toxic waste dump. In your shoes, I'd just quit.*

Mike's eyes flutter shut as his stream stays strong.

He laughs again.

Don't believe me? Hell, I quit on things all the time. Ask anybody. It's sort of what I'm known for.

He hears a louder pattering of urine and realizes his stream has gone astray. Opening his eyes, he shifts the stream back to the center of the toilet bowl. By then it's finally beginning to taper off ever so slightly. A helpless shiver goes through him as he groans in relief.

It takes him another moment to realize how cold it's gotten in the bathroom. That shiver isn't just a byproduct of physical relief. It's also gotten a bit darker in the small space. Not significantly so, but enough to notice. It's as if someone slightly turned down a dimmer switch. Only there's no dimmer switch in here. A quick glance at the light switch by the door confirms this. Yep. Just a regular old up-and-down number.

He frowns.

Huh. Weird.

Maybe the bulb in the ceiling light is close to burning out.

Whatever.

His piss stream at long last slows to a trickle and then ends after a last shake or two. Zipping up, he moves carefully over to the wash basin, still wary of the slippery floor. Unsurprisingly, the basin is less than spotlessly clean. He looks at the mirror above the sink and sees a booger smeared across the middle of the cracked glass.

Ugh.

Then he gasps as he glimpses something far more upsetting than a piece of dried mucus. Instead of his own reflection, he sees the face of a much older man staring back at him. This other person has an unruly mop of silver hair and an aged face that is hideously bloated and red. The vision is gone almost as soon as he takes a startled step backward.

Uncontrollable tremors rack his body as he stares distrustingly at the reflected image of his own face again. The heavy thudding of his heart feels like a wrecking ball against the wall of his chest. He feels precariously unsteady on his feet, like he might topple over at any moment. There's perspiration on his forehead despite the deepening chill in the bathroom. He laughs nervously because it's funny how genuinely frightened he feels now. Such a strange contrast to the total absence of fear he experienced while facing down those shotguns.

He tells himself what he saw in the mirror wasn't real.

No fucking way is that even possible.

A likely explanation suggests itself. He's pretty woozy from all the booze tonight. He was probably unconscious on his feet for a fraction of a second, maybe even a few whole seconds, and during that time his brain conjured up that horrible nightmare fragment. Nothing mysterious about it.

He lets out a slow breath and again approaches the basin, pausing there a moment to closely study the cracked reflective glass, ready to bolt from the room should the vision appear again. When several seconds elapse without that happening, he pumps some soap into his hands from the basin dispenser and turns on the hot water tap. He gets his next big shock the instant his hands are immersed in water.

The water isn't hot.

It's not even lukewarm.

Instead, it's freezing cold. Not regular cold like you might sometimes get from a hot water tap before the water warms up. No, this is more like how water trapped beneath a frozen shelf of arctic ice would feel.

He screeches and jerks his hands out of the water. "Holy shit, what the hell?"

As he utters these words, a fine mist emerges from his mouth and floats in the air a moment before dispersing. The mist appears again the next time he exhales. He shivers and finds himself wishing for a jacket. The temperature in the bathroom, still plummeting, feels as if it's gone down by at least another ten degrees within the last minute. It's also another few shades darker, as if someone turned down that imaginary dimmer switch even more. His reflection in the mirror now resembles a shadowy specter.

He swallows a lump in his throat and thinks, *Fuck it, I'm outta here.*

He wipes his wet hands on his pants and goes to the door. The doorknob is cold to the touch, like a baseball-shaped piece of ice. His palm starts to turn numb as he grips it more firmly and tries to turn it. At this point, the unnatural cold doesn't surprise him. What does surprise him is the doorknob's failure to yield to the pressure he exerts. It doesn't budge at all. Not even the tiniest fraction of an inch. It's as if it's welded shut. He continues trying to turn the knob a few moments longer, well after recognizing the futility of the effort.

RACING WITH THE DEVIL

Screeching in frustration, he lets go of the knob and pounds the base of a fist against the door, putting all his strength into it. Crazy as it seems, he doesn't think he's getting out of here without help. After banging away at the door with no response from anyone outside, he starts shouting, calling out to his friends with as much volume as he can muster.

He waits in vain in hopes of hearing their voices coming back this way. Waits to hear footsteps approaching from the other side. Neither of these things occur. Terror floods his system with adrenaline and he starts screaming, banging both fists against the immoveable door while his heart gallops. He keeps screaming until his voice turns hoarse. Tears cut icy rivulets down his reddening face. He sniffles as clouds of steamy breath waft from his mouth.

In the midst of his distress, an absurd possibility rises to the forefront of his mind. The bathroom is haunted. Probably the whole store is, which might explain the eerie emptiness of the place. Despite his interest in horror films, he's never believed in ghosts or the existence of any type of paranormal phenomenon. And yet he can't deny what his senses are telling him. He's definitely not asleep now. Despite the deep strangeness of what's happening, no dream has ever felt this real. This is actually fucking happening and he has no idea how to extract himself from the terrifying situation. He needs the help of an exorcist or someone with experience in banishing spirits, only he has no means of contacting any such person.

He thinks about his friends.

Wonders if they'll ever come check on him.

Please come get me out of here. Please, please.

He's close to total despair when he feels a gust of cold air stirring his hair, followed by more icy tendrils of it tickling his face. It becomes so cold in the bathroom his teeth actually start to chatter. A sound from somewhere behind him startles him. It's something he recognizes, a nature sound, the hooting of an owl. Definitely not something he should be hearing in a gas station bathroom. A deep dread settles within him like a heavy weight. He doesn't want to see what's behind him, but he knows he has to turn around and look.

Before doing that, however, he spends a few more moments staring at the door in front of him, reassuring himself of its essential reality. It looks the same as it always has. An ordinary door. It's not melting or shrouded in a shimmery mist, as might happen in a scary movie. He reaches out and places a hand flat against the door's metal surface. He almost sobs in relief when he feels the cold metal against his skin. The door is there. It physically exists. He glances at the coin-operated condom dispenser mounted on the wall next to the door.

Most of the condoms available for purchase are of the novelty variety. "Ribbed for her pleasure" reads the image above one selection, which also shows the face of a woman with big brunette hair and pouty red lips. She looks like a '70s porn actress. He reaches out and touches her image with the tip of a finger. The condom dispenser is as solid as the door. He takes his finger away and looks at the woman's lustful expression, feeling a pang of angst. What he wouldn't give to have those cherry lips wrapped around his dick right now. In some other, much warmer location than this goddamn haunted bathroom, obviously. Not that wishing for things he can't have has ever done him much good.

He sighs and slowly turns around.

He then stares in astonished silence at the open space where the opposite wall stood the last time he faced that direction. The wall is gone. The rest of the bathroom remains. The other walls. The disgusting toilet. The frozen piss on the floor. That untrustworthy mirror. But that back wall no longer exists. What he sees instead is a narrow and shadowy path through a dense stretch of forest. There's also some fog floating around out there, though it's not especially thick. He hears the hooting of that owl again, louder and perhaps a bit more agitated now.

My mind has cracked, Mike thinks. *That's the only thing that makes sense. A psychotic break. Of course. I'm crazy. That's all.*

He laughs, but there's a flatness to the sound.

He doesn't really believe he's crazy.

Yet what else could explain this?

What he's seeing now is several steps beyond his conception of how an actual haunting would manifest in reality. The supernatural phenomena occurring within a haunted structure should not extend beyond the physical bounds of that structure. Of course, once again, his assumptions in this area are based solely on what he's seen in movies. He has no genuine expertise in this area.

He turns toward the door again and tests the knob one last time.

It still doesn't budge.

Not knowing what else to do, he turns away from the door and approaches the open space where the back wall once stood. Another idea occurs to him, one he understands he must test before starting down that shadowy path into the woods. He hardly dares to hope for anything good to happen at this point, but maybe the solution to his dilemma is a simple one.

He approaches the still-standing section of wall to his right and peeks around it. A deflating sense of disappointment makes him groan. He thought he might be able to just step around that section of wall and walk back out to the parking lot, but it's immediately clear that won't be an option. He sees nothing of the store's exterior, nor any clear way back out to the parking lot. All he sees is more trees where the store should be.

He calls out to his missing friends again as a last-ditch move.

As expected by now, he gets no response.

Giving up, Mike steps fully out of the bathroom and starts down the foggy path.

NINE

DENNIS COMES OUT OF THE store and sees Steve leaning against the Camaro with an open can of Bud gripped in his right hand. There's no sign of the beer cartons he and Dave pilfered from the store, so those must already be stashed away in the car. There's also no sign of Dave. Good bet he's slumped down in the backseat, passed out again from overindulgence.

"Are you crazy, man?" Dennis inquires as he steps off the sidewalk and approaches his car. "I know this is a quiet spot, but drinking right out in the open still isn't a great idea."

An unexpected look of deep exasperation creases Steve's features right before he takes a big gulp from the can. "What can I say, motherfucker, I got bored. You fucking disappeared."

Dennis gives him a slack-jawed look of uncomprehending confusion for a moment before shaking his head. "The fuck are you talking about? *Disappeared?*" He enunciates the word with thick, disdainful emphasis. "I didn't *disappear*, goddammit. I poked around in that storeroom a couple minutes, tops, and came right back out."

Now it's Steve's turn to stare blankly at him for a prolonged silent moment. Then he abruptly takes another big swig of beer and angrily tosses the can away. It rolls away on the asphalt, trailing a surprising amount of foamy liquid from the opening. Wasting a half-finished brew is not like Steve at all. He'd ordinarily consider such a thing sacrilege.

Jesus, Dennis thinks. *He must really be pissed the fuck off.*

But about what?

Steve takes a few quick strides toward him, until they're standing a few feet apart. Up close, his anger is even more evident. The quivering of his jawline. The flaring of his nostrils. He looks like he's about to erupt.

"Look, asshole," he says, jabbing a shaking forefinger at Dennis. "I don't know what kind of fucked-up game you fuckers are playing, but I've fucking had it. It's time to stop. Right goddamn now."

Dennis has never seen his friend anywhere near this enraged about anything. Unfortunately, his confusion has only deepened. He again experiences that unsettling sense of the uncanny that gripped him during his brief time in the storeroom. Something isn't right about this. Something is *off*. His stomach starts twisting as he stares in perplexion at Steve's angry visage.

"Game? I don't ... what are you ... ?" Dennis trails off and heaves an exasperated breath. "Game? What do you mean by that?"

Steve snorts. "Knock it off with the innocent act. You know exactly what I mean. Yeah, I *know* you were in the storeroom. I saw you go in there. But you never came out again until just fucking now."

Dennis laughs haltingly, a nervous sound brought on by stress. It is entirely devoid of actual amusement. "Please help me understand, man. I'm begging you. How is that any different from what I just said?"

Steve's mouth curls as he makes a sound of disgust. He goes back over to the Camaro and leans in through the open window, reaching into the back for a moment before backing out again with a fresh can of Bud. Foam rushes from the opening as he pops the tab. It's perhaps the most agitated opening of a beer can Dennis has ever seen. Steve puts the can to his mouth and guzzles deeply from it before taking it away again.

This can also gets tossed away half-consumed. Steve wipes foam from his mouth and laughs in a bitter way. "Motherfucker, you weren't gone just a couple minutes. Wherever the fuck you actually went after the storeroom, you were there over half a fucking hour. At least."

Dennis frowns again. "Bullshit. That's not possible."

Steve sneers. "I swear I'm telling the absolute goddamn truth." He holds up an open-palmed hand like a trial witness about to get sworn in. "Check the clock in your car if you don't fucking believe me."

Dennis holds his friend's gaze a bit longer, praying he'll soon see cracks appear in that red-faced veneer. Clinging to the increasingly slim hope this is all about to be revealed as an elaborate prank. It doesn't feel that way at all, but what is the alternative here?

Believing anything else can lead only to madness.

He lets out a breath and says, "Okay. I'll check."

Steve laughs in that bitter way again, but says nothing. There's what Dennis can only think of as a *knowing* look on his face. It radiates rock-solid confidence in having his wild claim verified. The expression is nearly as unsettling as anything else that's happened so far.

Dennis goes around to the other side of the car and slides in behind the wheel after opening the door. He jabs the key in the ignition slot and turns it forward to turn on the radio and light up the dash. He stares at the digital numbers on the radio clock and feels that tightening in his stomach getting worse. The time displayed is a good forty minutes later than he was expecting. It's even more time than Steve thought had elapsed.

He takes the key out of the ignition and gets out of the car again, standing just outside of it with the door part way open. Steve is watching him over the roof, smirking even harder now. Dennis is on the verge of admitting he's wrong about the time elapsed—as impossible to understand as that is—when he's distracted by something else. A belated recognition of something else off-kilter. He ducks his head down again and peers into the Camaro's backseat, staring at the empty space for several seconds.

Then he raises his head again and looks at Steve. "Where's Dave?"

Steve tilts his head slightly, his eyes narrowing. "Who the fuck is Dave?"

Dennis studies his friend's expression for a few silent moments. His chest feels tight, like it sometimes does after eating too much spicy food, but this isn't heartburn. It's another manifestation of dread. His breath starts quickening. This is all too much, this strange shit that keeps happening. He wonders if he might start hyperventilating. Once again, there is no hint of deception in the look on Steve's face. He looks puzzled. And not in the agitated way of minutes ago. It's the way anyone might look upon hearing a casual reference to someone they don't know and have never met.

His head swivels about as he searches the parking lot for any sign of Dave Robinson. Maybe he's hiding somewhere. Maybe there's still a chance this is just the most fucked-up prank of all time. But Dave is nowhere in sight, nor are there any obvious places to hide, unless he's gone around behind the store.

Dennis thinks of something else as his gaze returns to Steve. "Hold on. Just hold the fuck on."

He presses a hand to his chest, willing his heart to stop pounding so hard. He's thinking of something else Steve said shortly after he came out of the store. *I don't know what kind of fucked-up game you fuckers are playing* . . .

Fuckers. Plural.

"Where's Mike?"

For one painfully tense moment, he's certain Steve will show him that mildly puzzled look again and say, "Who's Mike?"

Steve grimaces.

This time it isn't simple confusion Dennis reads in his expression. It's anguish.

He lifts his hands in a gesture of helplessness and shakes his head. "Dude, I don't fucking know. He went into the bathroom and as far as I can tell never came out again, which obviously isn't actually fucking possible, but I can't for the life of me figure out where he really went. I waited and waited for you guys to come back out, but you never did. Well, *you* finally did, after a long-ass time. I gave up waiting at one point and went back in to drag your asses back out here. Only I couldn't find you. *Anywhere.*"

His eyes are shiny with tears he's struggling to hold back.

Dennis is silent for a moment as he thinks things over.

Coming to no conclusions—as if he could—he bends down again and extracts two cans of Bud from the carton in back. He notes there's just the one case, almost certainly the one Steve pinched. Of course, he knows there should be at least one more of those cardboard cartons back there, but the other ones seem to have vanished from existence along with Dave.

He takes the wet cans around to the other side of the car, offering one to Steve, who accepts it with a heavy sigh of gratitude. The cans fizz as they pop them open and take silent, contemplative swigs.

Steve sniffles after taking a second, smaller sip. "Dude . . . what's going on here? Like, seriously . . . what the fuck?"

Dennis shrugs. "I don't know. I'm sorry, but I really don't. It's something not natural, though. Don't think there's much doubt about that."

He takes another slow look around, wishing with all his heart to see Mike and Dave suddenly materializing out of the inky, suffocating darkness. But of course that doesn't happen. A heartbreaking conviction takes hold of him.

They'll never see either of those guys again.

He's about to ask Steve for more details regarding his search of the store while he was "missing" when he begins to hear the rumble of an approaching engine. It's the first hint of any other human presence in the area and he automatically turns toward the sound. At the same time, he realizes there's something disquietingly familiar about it.

He looks out at the street and sees nothing at first, but the sound grows louder and soon bright headlights appear in the distance. The engine revs loudly and the car races down the street, nearing the store within seconds. There's music blaring from the oncoming automobile, AC/DC's "Highway to Hell," cranked up to earth-shaking volume.

Tires squeal as the car abruptly swings into the parking lot.

Dennis lets out a resigned breath.

Of course, he thinks. *Of course it's you again.*

The black Z28 slows down and rolls to a stop a few feet away from them.

TEN

SEVERAL MINUTES AFTER SETTING OFF down the narrow, winding path in the woods, Mike stops and turns around, looking back in the direction from which he came. The exposed interior of the haunted bathroom was still visible the first time he stopped and glanced backward, but that is no longer the case. It's obscured now by the floating mist and the twisting of the path. Or at least that's the reason basic logic suggests. Now, however, he wonders if he'd even be able to find it again if he tried retracing his steps. He suspects the answer is no, if only because normal logic clearly does not apply to his situation.

He thinks if he goes back that way he'll end up hopelessly lost, a confused and directionless wanderer in an increasingly phantasmagorical landscape. Some otherworldly force is at work here, one wishing to guide him in a particular direction. Whether that force is doing so toward some nefarious purpose he doesn't know, but he strongly suspects it isn't acting as some protective guardian. Even so, he believes the path revealed to him by the disappearance of the bathroom wall was no random occurrence. And if he's meant to continue in the direction he's been going, whether for purposes benign or otherwise, he might as well see this journey through to the end.

The only way out is through.

With a sigh, he turns around again and resumes walking down the path.

Mike walks and walks for what feels like a long time. All the while, the path continues to snake about this way and that, never at any point turning into anything resembling a straight line. The higher branches of the trees lining the path are barren of leaves, allowing him to look up at the clear night sky with its vista of twinkling stars. Perhaps because he's alone in a strange and unknown place, he experiences an aching sense of awe he normally doesn't when taking in the same view under ordinary circumstances. The sky is always there. The stars are always there. Maybe he felt something like this when he looked up at them as a kid, but not often since then. He feels small and insignificant. It hits him that in the grand scheme of things his entire existence—all his hopes, dreams, and disappointments—doesn't really mean much at all.

What does it really matter if he never makes it back out of the woods? The answer is obvious. It doesn't matter. If he never emerges from this strange stretch of nightmare country, his family and friends will mourn his mysterious loss, but the rest of the world—the rest of the whole universe—will not care one bit. He'll be gone forever and his memory will fade even in the minds of those who loved him the most. Then eventually they'll die and take their faded recollections of him with them, and then it'll be as if he never existed at all.

And so what?

The world will carry on without him, unaffected utterly.

More time passes.

An hour or more.

And yet he never starts to feel winded, as he ordinarily would when traipsing through the woods for such a long time. Even stranger after all the beer he slammed back earlier, he's never overcome with an urgent need to stop and piss again. This is odd enough to cause him to wonder if somehow he died back at that gas station and now he's just wandering through some form of purgatory. The idea is hard to dismiss outright given the strangeness of everything, but other factors make him doubt this theory. There's too much evidence of other physical processes still functioning normally. The constant misting of his breath as he inhales and exhales cold air. The gooseflesh on his arms. The occasional need to scratch an itch. He's gone long enough between beers for his buzz to fade considerably, but it hasn't completely gone away.

Just when he starts to believe this path might truly be endless, his ears begin to perceive a faint sound of music. Amplified electric rock music. At first he fears the sound is an aural hallucination brought on by a mixture of dread and weariness from his long walk, but the sound doesn't go away. The source is still a ways off in the distance, but he's certain it's real and not the illusory product of an overstressed brain pushed to the breaking point. Because of the distance, the sound is too faint to identify the actual song being played, but something about it makes him believe he's hearing live music rather than a recording.

Mike quickens his pace, accelerating to a point just shy of a jog. The music gets slowly but steadily louder. Soon the notes he's hearing become imbued with a tantalizing familiarity. He's sure he's only moments away from being able to recognize it.

Then it comes to him.

"Walk This Way" by Aerosmith.

The live band is aces and the singer is doing a dead-on Steven Tyler impression.

Mike can't help it. He laughs.

It's too perfect, like a soundtrack cue in a movie. Probably it's only a coincidence, but maybe not. This is simply too strange a night to dismiss anything that feels meaningful as mere coincidence.

RACING WITH THE DEVIL

The closer he gets to the source of the music, the more he becomes aware of other noises filtering through the blare of amplified rock and roll. Again, he needs a few additional moments to recognize what he's hearing. Then recognition dawns. It's a babble of voices, the generalized drone of a crowd, the sound you hear in a concert arena before the show begins.

There are people somewhere up ahead of him. A significant number, from the sound of things. And not too far away now at all. This path isn't endless, after all. He smiles as relief explodes within him and breaks into a run, anxious to be out of these woods and back in the company of human beings. He craves the restoration of something resembling ordinary life, some stark refutation of the state of existential surrender that gripped him earlier. The fog begins to retreat as his feet chew up the ground. There aren't quite so many tall trees lining the path the closer he gets to the outdoor concert or whatever this gathering is.

He laughs as he sees the end of the path up ahead.

Salvation is within reach, at long last.

He emerges into a large open field and comes to an abrupt dead stop.

As he suspected, the music is courtesy of a live band. They're performing on a long flatbed trailer parked in the approximate center of the field, which is large enough to accommodate a big football stadium with some room left over. The terrain has the look of farm acreage that has fallen into disuse, an easy guess based on the presence of a barn off in the distance, the dark outline of which stands well beyond where the band is jamming away on the flatbed. Speaking of the band, they've transitioned from Aerosmith to Black Sabbath, playing "Paranoid" as Mike stands there gawking at the edge of the field.

At a guess, there are hundreds of people at this gathering. They're not all standing together in front of the band the way they would be at an arena. Instead, they're either wandering around in a seemingly aimless way or hanging out in groups scattered across the field. A lot of them are hanging out around bonfires and keg stations. Unsurprisingly, many have drinks in their hands. Cans, bottles, and plastic cups filled with beer from the kegs. As he surveys the varied other hedonistic activities taking place, he catches sight of what looks like a mud pit. He squints in that direction and in a few moments realizes the dark forms squirming around in the pit are large-breasted young women covered in mud. They're wrestling in a no-holds-barred, aggressive manner. It's a captivating sight, but he keeps looking around because the mud pit is far from the only unusual thing here.

There's another naked woman over by the nearest bonfire. The only thing she's wearing is a pointed black witch's hat. She's swaying about to the music with her eyes closed and one of those plastic beer cups grasped loosely in her right hand. The hat looks like something she probably picked up at a Spencer Gifts store in the mall. Loads of other people have donned masks depicting various horror film icons, most prominent among them of course being Jason Voorhees, Freddy Kreuger, and Leatherface. The masks are of varying quality. A few look quite expensive, as if they were produced in a limited quantity in the lab of a makeup FX professional, while others are terrible-looking cheap plastic crap from Walgreens or K-Mart. A smaller but still significant number of people are decked out in elaborate full costumes, including one guy who's a dead ringer for Christopher Lee in *Dracula Has Risen from the Grave*. There are werewolves, mummies, and beer-swilling zombies.

Taken all together, it's a panorama of sheer Halloween awesomeness.

Something occurs to Mike then.

This is the epic spook night party in the boonies Darryl Frykowski told them about earlier. It seems Dennis was wrong about it being something that existed only in the burnout's drug-addled imagination. In that moment of recognition, his most fervent wish is for his friends to be here with him. They should see and experience this, too.

Maybe it's not too late.

Maybe he should hurry back to the gas station and fetch them.

He glances behind him and sees that the path out of the woods has vanished. As he stares at the spot where it should be, he experiences a recurrence of his prior uneasiness. He thinks again of the haunted bathroom and the disappearance of his friends. For a time, as he initially drank in the intoxicating sights and sounds of the party, his troubles were far from his mind. Now they're intruding again and he doesn't like it one bit.

The band plays on, the strains of "Ziggy Stardust" resonating in the night.

When the song ends, Mike stops looking for the missing path and ventures forward into the party.

Soon he has a plastic cup brimming with beer in his hand.

He drains it and has another.

And another one after that. And so on.

Getting fucked the fuck up as the band plays deep into the night.

ELEVEN

AFTER EXCHANGING AN UNEASY GLANCE, Dennis and Steve both take an instinctive step backward. The music has ceased blaring from the black Z28, but the powerful engine is still rumbling in idle. Dennis dislikes showing anything resembling fear in the presence of an obvious aggressor, but something primal has overridden the bravado he normally defaults to when confronted or backed into a corner. The Z got so close to them before coming to a stop. It makes him think of the way a schoolyard bully will sometimes get right up in the face of the kid he's picking on, seeking to terrify them into begging for mercy.

The sleek black automobile looks like a sentient, predatory beast. Dennis stares at it with a sense of grim disappointment as he waits for the unseen driver to do something. He was hoping he'd left the Z behind for good with his high-speed evasive driving techniques, taking multiple sharp-angled sudden turns down side streets, but it appears he was wrong. Then again, maybe the Z showing up here is just a case of cosmic bad luck. Or they've simply lingered in this spot too long while the Z continued to prowl these dark roads in search of them.

Whatever the case, how this moment of final confrontation came about doesn't matter. Dennis is now convinced this is simply the workings of fate, something that's been inevitable from the beginning.

He grits his teeth and his hands tighten into fists at his sides.

Okay, fucker, he thinks. *Let's do this.*

He then thinks of the aluminum baseball bat in the trunk of his car, wondering if he has time to grab it before anything happens. Ordinarily in fight situations he relies on his fists. He's no Mike Tyson. He's not invincible. But he's come out on top in these scenarios more often than not. This time, though, he's up against an opponent he fears he might not be able to best by normal means, which is a strange way to feel given that he still doesn't truly know what he's up against here. For all he knows, the Z's driver is a pipsqueak, some guy with small dick syndrome who thinks driving a badass car makes him tougher than he really is. All he's seen so far is the slender arm of the driver's female companion right before she threw that beer bottle. Those goddamn tinted windows have hidden everything else.

There's a squeaking of hinges as the doors of the Z finally begin to open. Dennis feels a sharp pang of regret at not acting faster to retrieve the baseball bat. Well, there's nothing he can do about it now. He doesn't want to go scrambling for it in the last moment like a scared little bitch. All he can do now is play the hand dealt him and hope for the best.

The first person to emerge from the Z is the girl riding shotgun. The same one who threw the beer bottle. She directs a smirk at him as she approaches the store in an unhurried, carefree way. Her choppy-looking short hair is dyed midnight-black. She wears a tiny black leather jacket over a midriff-exposing black top, a miniskirt, and fishnets. There's a large Motorhead patch on the back of the jacket.

Her heels clack on the asphalt as she walks with a hip-swaying swagger. Her pale flesh looks as if it hasn't been touched by the sun in years. She looks like a rock and roll ghost.

She cuts such a compelling figure that Dennis and Steve both fail to immediately notice the emergence of the driver. Their heads snap back toward the Z when they hear an amused chuckle.

Dennis chokes back a gulp upon first seeing his adversary.

The Z's driver stands slouched against the side of his car with his muscular arms folded over his chest. His current posture makes it difficult to accurately gauge his height, but Dennis guesses it's more than six feet by at least a couple of inches. He wears black jeans, a sleeveless black muscle tee, and black motorcycle boots. There's an Elmer Fudd tattoo on his right bicep. His shoulder-length brown hair is worn in an outdated '70s feather cut. Black sunglasses obscure his eyes. While the driver and his punk rock girlfriend share an obvious wardrobe preference, they diverge in terms of skin pallor. His skin has a strange gray-ish hue with mottled patches of blue and green.

Dennis frowns. "Is that . . . makeup? Are you supposed to be a fucking zombie?"

The driver chuckles in that amused way again and shrugs. "I get why you'd think that. It *is* Halloween, after all." His smile fades and he regards Dennis silently from behind his sunglasses for a moment. "Look close, Dennis. Does it really look like makeup to you?"

Dennis scowls at the man's use of his name. "Do I know you?"

The Z's driver shrugs again. "In a way, everybody knows me."

A statement that clears up exactly nothing as far as Dennis is concerned. He waits for the stranger to elaborate. When that doesn't happen, he studies the man's mottled features more closely, searching them for anything familiar. He doesn't think he actually knows this person, but the guy's not a mind reader. Telepaths only exist in Stephen King novels.

"Looks like you took a bath in a barrel of radioactive waste, you ugly fuck," Steve interjects, snickering as he glances over at Dennis.

"Dumb son of a bitch must think he's Corey Hart, wearing his sunglasses at night."

Dennis smirks. "Yeah. And what's with the Farrah Fawcett hair? You do know it's not 1977 anymore, right?"

He feels bolstered by his friend's snide tone, which is devoid of even the faintest detectable trace of fear. If his friend isn't afraid, maybe he doesn't have to be either, despite the stranger's unnerving use of his name. And as for that, there doesn't have to be any sinister reason behind it. Maybe one night the guy was hanging out in the same bar he was and simply overheard someone addressing him as Dennis. Easy enough explanation. Sure, anyone remembering a random person's name like that is unusual, but it's far from impossible.

The man in the sunglasses laughs. "Those are some good ones, fellas. Some serious burns, truly. As for what year it is, well, that's not as cut and dry as you think. In your world, sure, it sort of is, but you've wandered into some strange territory. *My* territory. And out here time isn't such a linear thing. Heck, it doesn't really exist as you understand it at all."

Dennis and Steve stare at him in perplexed silence a moment before again exchanging confused, wary glances.

Dennis shakes his head slowly. "Time doesn't exist? Are you stupid? What the fuck is that supposed to mean?"

The man sighs. "I never said time doesn't exist. You should pay attention better." He comes out of his slouching posture as he pushes away from the Z28 and turns fully toward them. "What I actually said was time doesn't exist out here as *you* understand it. And what that means, Dennis, is it doesn't go in a straight line. Depending on the route you take, you could end up back in 1987, the year it was when you and your pals embarked on your ill-fated adventure. But you might also wind up in 1977. Or 2021. The possibilities are endless."

Dennis gapes at him, unsure what to say.

The guy is insane.

Steve makes a loud sound of rude derision. "Man, fuck this.

Dude's full of shit. He's messing with us and I'm tired of listening to the garbage coming out of his stupid fucking mouth. Let's either kick his fucking ass or get out of here."

The stranger laughs.

Before he can respond to this provocation any other way, the girl comes out of the store again, her approach heralded by the clacking of her heels. She again aims a smirking glance at Dennis and Steve as she swaggers by them. Wedged into a corner of her mouth is an unlit cigarette. As she struts across the parking lot, she lights it from a silver Zippo, which she then snaps shut with impressive flair. She is, in every way, Dennis's idea of the ultimate embodiment of cool. In her presence, he feels compelled to project an aura of unruffled aloofness. He can't help it. It's an instinct embedded so deeply within his DNA no other response is even possible.

She sets a case of beer on the hood of the Z28. Turning toward them, she holds the cigarette pinched between two fingers of an upraised hand, with wispy smoke curling away from the glowing tip. "Look at that one," she says, tilting her chin to indicate Dennis. "He's trying so hard to look tough and fearless. It's adorable."

The Z's driver glances at her. "Now, now, Nora. Don't make fun of him. He can't help it. You know how young boys are around you."

The girl he called Nora puffs on her cigarette and shrugs. "I'm not making fun of him. I really do think it's cute. It makes all this so much sadder than it already is."

Dennis glares at them. "I'm not a young boy. I'm twenty-two. A grown fucking man."

Steve groans. "Dude, stop letting them get under your skin. It's like I said, they're messing with us. Let's fucking *go*, okay?"

The stranger's head swivels toward him. "You're not going anywhere, Steve. Not now or ever again. For you, the party's over, sad to say."

"Fuck this."

Steve takes a run at him.

The move is pure Steve Wade, a tactic Dennis has seen him use numerous times. Because he isn't big, he attempts to compensate by charging at opponents and driving them to the ground. If he can do that and get on top of them, he can overwhelm them with a flurry of hard punches to the face. Sometimes it works and other times it doesn't. In this case, of course, Dennis will be backing him up within seconds. The stranger's size is intimidating—as is his muscular build—but it's two against one. Yeah, there's the girl to consider, but she's small and probably won't insert herself in a fight between three pissed off dudes.

They can take him down.

Maybe.

But the stranger never even flinches as Steve barrels toward him. Instead, he holds out the flat of a hand and Steve's forehead runs smack into it. His momentum does not push the man's hand backward or move him in any other perceptible way. And judging from the relaxed set of his features, he's exerting little discernible physical effort at all. He's holding Steve back as easily as he'd deflect a mosquito. Even stranger, Steve makes no attempt to spin away from the intercepting hand. In fact, he doesn't move at all. He's frozen in place as perfectly as a prehistoric bug trapped in amber. Even the tail of his trench coat looks frozen, hanging perfectly still in the air, caught in mid-flap.

Dennis trembles as he finally accepts what he should have known all along. The stranger is no ordinary man. He might not even be human. Maybe he's something else wearing a man's body like a suit. Or a costume. That might explain the mottled flesh, which Dennis now accepts isn't ordinary skin slathered in cheap Halloween makeup.

It looks like it does because it's rotting.

The stranger takes his hand away from Steve's forehead. As soon as the physical connection between them is broken, Steve is frozen no longer. He crumples to the ground and doesn't move.

Anguish swelling within him, Dennis rushes over to his friend and drops to a knee at his side. Steve landed face-down on the asphalt. Dennis grabs hold of him and flips him over, wincing and grunting at the unresponsive dead weight, feeling sick at the way his arm flops back to the pavement. He checks for a pulse and is shocked by how cold his skin feels. He holds a hand over Steve's open mouth, hoping to feel a warm rush of breath, but there's nothing.

Fighting back tears, he looks up at the strangers, glancing first at Nora before glaring at her inhuman companion. "What did you do to him?"

The man with the rotting skin regards him impassively. "Getting pissed at me is pointless, son. He was already gone. He just didn't know it yet."

Dennis takes a steadying breath and gets slowly to his feet.

This creature wearing the flesh of a man knows things he shouldn't know. This is a disturbing thing on its own, but he's insinuating things that are even more unsettling. Things a protective part of his psyche would prefer not to examine too closely, but Dennis fights this instinct. Shrinking away from grim reality will accomplish exactly nothing. So many things he doesn't understand have happened. Maybe the stranger can shed some light on them.

Like . . .

"Why didn't he remember Dave?"

The stranger's infuriatingly smug smile returns. "Oh, that. Steve didn't forget about Dave Robinson. Not in the normal way one forgets things, anyway. You can chalk that up to the brain damage."

Dennis frowns. "Brain damage? What are you talking about? He was fine until . . ." He falls silent a moment as he realizes he doesn't quite have the right words for what he wants to say. The moment Steve met his fate is still gut-wrenchingly vivid in his mind, but it remains far beyond his ability to comprehend. His only means of articulating what he saw is the simplest way possible. "He was fine until you touched him."

The stranger shakes his head. "I know how it looked, but that's simply not true. Look, kid, I get the desire for enlightenment, but knowledge doesn't always bring peace." He laughs as he tears open the beer carton Nora brought out of the store and takes out a can of Lowenbrau. "Listen to me, I sound like a fucking hippie with this peace and enlightenment garbage."

Nora smirks and also takes a can out of the carton. "Ugh. Gag me with a fucking spoon. You wouldn't be nearly as hot in bell bottoms and tie-dye."

Dennis wants to scoff, but says nothing.

Does this chick seriously find the thing in the rotting flesh suit "hot"? He supposes he could see it before the decay began, but now? She must be as twisted as he is, albeit in ways not as immediately obvious.

The stranger grabs her and pulls her close. They kiss hungrily in protracted fashion, their mouths opening on occasion, allowing him glimpses of their tongues tangling. Hers is pink and healthy-looking. His is a sick shade of swollen gray. It goes on long enough to make him uncomfortable, a feeling that escalates considerably when Nora starts moaning in a sexual way.

Dennis loudly clears his throat.

They break their clench with obvious reluctance, their faces turning slowly toward him.

Dennis sighs. "You weird assholes can go get a fucking room somewhere if you're that horny. Or, hell, do it in your creepy-ass car. But it'd be awesome if you could finish explaining yourself first."

The stranger pops the tab on his Lowenbrau as he stands up straight again. "You need to take what I said to heart, boy. Enlightenment won't make you feel better. Quite the fucking opposite is true in this case, I'm afraid. Here's all I'm interested in telling you. Dave is gone because he's *gone*. Understand? He was the first of you to succumb. That's why you never saw him again. Steve was able to hang on a little longer. That's why he was able to be with you here for a short time. But they're both lost to you now. Forever."

Dennis feels tears welling in his eyes again. "What about Mike?"

The stranger takes a swig of beer and wipes his mouth. "What about him?"

"Is he . . . ?" Dennis feels his heart swell as a sob tries to rise up in his throat. "Is he dead, too?"

The stranger frowns and appears to give the matter some real thought this time. It's the first time he hasn't appeared completely confident in the secrets locked inside his head. He takes another swig of beer and shrugs. "Okay, I admit it. Him I'm not so sure about. He seems to have wandered into a place beyond my reach. I can't see him. But if it's any consolation, I don't *think* he's dead. At least not yet."

Dennis clings to the sliver of hope implicit in this admission.

He sighs. "And me? Am I . . . ?"

The stranger shakes his head. "No. Not yet. And actually, that brings us to why we're having this little chat. I'm gonna be honest with you here, Denny. You're a borderline case. Not as immediately critical as your unfortunate friends, but you're in rough shape. It could go either way for you, depending on how quickly help arrives. I'm offering you a chance to improve your odds."

"How?"

The stranger laughs heartily. "How? It's simple. *This is my realm.*" His intonation is thunderous, like the bellow of a barbarian. He spreads his arms wide and turns in a slow circle, chuckling as he faces Dennis again. "My domain. And I hold significant sway here. I can even influence events in your world to some degree. And I'm willing to do that for you if you do something for me."

Dennis feels a queasy wariness upon hearing those words. He doesn't trust this guy—this creature or demon, whatever he actually is—but he doesn't have a lot of options here. Not any good ones, anyway.

"What do you want from me?"

The stranger smirks deeply as he steps closer, getting up to within a few feet of Dennis. "I challenge you to a race, kid." He laughs again and drinks more of his beer. "Oh, hell, let's just go ahead and call it a death race."

Nora cackles as she exhales another cloud of smoke.

They're both laughing their asses off now, as if the remark is the funniest shit they've ever heard.

At first, Dennis scowls.

Then he shows them the deranged grin of a condemned madman who knows there's no escaping his date with the hangman.

And is no longer afraid.

"All right, you laughing cunts. Let's fucking race."

TWELVE

AFTER DRAINING SEVERAL CUPS OF brew, Mike's buzz is back to a level he deems appropriate for a blowout beer bash on Halloween. He feels pleasantly light and even more pleasantly disconnected from his troubles. Deep in the back of his mind, he knows this unworried mood is temporary. There are horrors awaiting him when he's sober again, when the party is over and he's forced to leave this place. Traumatic, soul-scarring real-life horror. There will be no avoiding it, but for now it doesn't matter.

For now he feels like he's floating, borne aloft on a cloud of foamy suds, his feet barely touching the ground. He stops at various points and engages easily with various strangers. They laugh and dance together. He even makes out with the naked girl in the witch hat. It all feels so magical, like something from a perfect dream. Even in the midst of drunken debauchery at previous keggers, he's never felt quite this way before. Never so *free*. Not even close.

The only thing even mildly unsettling is the complete absence of anyone he knows or even just recognizes. He's been to a few of these outdoor rural throwdowns, but the scale of this one dwarfs them all. This is like the Halloween kegger version of Woodstock, and the attendees are all young, mostly high school or college age or a little older. The whole time he's wandering around, he never once sees anyone resembling a geezer. In theory, these are his peers. And they must all be from places nearby. He shouldn't be able to circulate in a crowd like this for any significant time without bumping into at least a few people he knows by sight, if not by name.

But it never happens.

It's an undeniably strange thing, but he's having too awesome a time to allow it to bother him much.

Not long after making out with the girl in the witch hat, he weaves away over to another of the many kegs scattered about the grounds of the party. This one is set up on the open tailgate of an old powder blue pickup truck. Several people are gathered around it, laughing and talking. Shooting the shit. There's one big, affable guy who's staked out a spot right next to the keg. He's wearing a blue football-type jersey. There's no number on the jersey, just the word "BEER" printed in block letters on the front. He's pouring beers for whoever comes up to the truck and loudly encouraging everyone to drink faster.

"*It ain't a party until somebody pukes!*" he proclaims several times.

After handing Mike a cup of freshly poured beer, the big guy gives him a wild-eyed look and says, "What about you, kemosabe? Have you puked yet?"

Mike laughs and shakes his head. "Not yet, but I'm sure I will before the night's over."

"You gotta get to work on that, my man. No rest for the wicked. Chug that fucking beer right now. Chug, chug, chug!"

The people gathered around the pickup truck take up the chant. *Chug! Chug! Chug!*

Mike smiles and thinks, *Fuck it, what the hell.*

He raises the cup to his mouth and drains it in what has to be close to record time for him.

The onlookers cheer and raise their own cups in the air.

The big guy turns his face to the sky and howls like a wolf, a sound so piercing it makes Mike wince slightly. Then the guy fixes him with that wild-eyed grin again and says, "It's Halloween, Mike. You gotta howl at the moon. Come on, howl with me."

The guy looks at the sky again and unleashes another of those piercing howls.

After a brief hesitation, Mike howls with him.

Seconds later, over there on the long flatbed trailer, the band launches into a version of Warren Zevon's "Werewolves of London," one that's considerably harder-rocking than the original. Many of the partiers howl along with the song at the appropriate moments, a raucously joyful bit of audience participation.

Mike wanders away from the pickup truck after getting yet another cup of beer. He decides to get closer to the flatbed trailer and spend a few minutes focusing on watching the band perform, something he hasn't done yet. Just listening to them from a distance has already convinced him they're the best cover band he's ever heard. Their takes on songs by other artists aren't always completely faithful to the originals, but they perform them with such energy and skill it doesn't matter.

As he starts making his way over there, he keeps an eye out for the girl in the witch hat. Earlier she told him she had to go see some friends but definitely wanted to spend some time with him later. This was said in a way that left him believing he stands a reasonable chance of getting laid before the end of the evening. It's another thing contributing significantly to his overall lightness of spirit. He looks forward to telling his friends all about it whenever they're all able to reconvene, hopefully sometime after daybreak. That he still has no idea where they are or how to make his way back to them is another matter he pushes to the back of his mind. It can wait.

RACING WITH THE DEVIL

He threads his way through the loose knot of people assembled in front of the trailer until he's standing at the front of the crowd. There's an open area of maybe ten feet between the edge of the trailer and the onlookers, many of whom are either bobbing their heads or dancing about drunkenly. The open area isn't roped off or blocked in any other way. The people watching seem content to hang back.

Mike is reminded of his second time seeing the Ramones. The first time was in a packed club of decent size. The crowd was raucous and into it in a big way, in part because it was the first time the legendary punk band played an area venue in several years. When they came around again and played a different, smaller club not even a year and a half later, it was much more sparsely attended. Mike spent the entire show standing six feet away from the Ramones while they performed on a tiny stage not truly fit for so mighty a band.

These memories are quickly dispersed as he takes in his first good, unobstructed look at this band. At first he's smiling and swaying to the music, but then his features slacken and his mouth begins to drop open. The first thing he notices is that one of the guitarists bears an uncanny resemblance to deceased Thin Lizzy frontman Phil Lynott. He thinks maybe the guitarist has made himself look like Lynott through a combination of makeup and attire, perhaps as some kind of rock and roll Halloween costume, but he only needs a few extra seconds of close scrutiny to realize that's not the case. This isn't just a close *resemblance*. Mike has all of Lizzy's albums on vinyl. He's spent enough time looking at the pictures on those record sleeves to recognize the man when he sees him.

The guitarist *is* Phil Lynott, impossible as that seems.

The man died not even two years ago, a victim of complications stemming from severe drug and alcohol dependency, but here he is, resurrected and performing on a fucking flatbed trailer in the middle of nowhere. In almost the precise instant this moment of recognition occurs, Lynott abruptly turns toward Mike as he's playing and makes direct eye contact.

A shiver goes through Mike as he averts his gaze and looks at the drummer, who has a distinctly powerful, propulsive playing style. The unwelcome intrusion of disquiet deepens and his good mood begins to sour.

The drummer is John Bonham, the deceased Led Zeppelin legend.

Mike looks at the singer and groans.

Bon fucking Scott. What the fuck is going on?

The bass player he doesn't recognize, but he thinks the other guitarist might be Tommy Bolin, though he's not sure about that. But at this point does it really matter?

This is a band of dead men.

He starts retreating into the crowd as the current song ends.

Bon Scott moves to the edge of the trailer and addresses the cheering onlookers. "Thank you, thank you. Me and the boys appreciate it. But now we'd like to turn your attention to tonight's guest of honor. His name is Mike Burnett and this is the worst night of his life. He's a shy one, so let's put a spotlight on the boy."

As soon as he says this, a bright light pops on somewhere overhead. Mike stops in his tracks and glances upward, squinting at the bright glowing circle high above him. Here's another thing that shouldn't be possible. He sees no cables or crane suspending the big spotlight. It's just floating there, held up by some unknown force. Fucking magic for all he knows. The other onlookers move away from him, forming a loose circle around him as the spotlight pins him in place.

His buoyant mood has entirely deserted him now. He feels queasy as bile touches the back of his throat. When he looks at the people surrounding him, he detects a strange and disturbing eagerness in the faces he can actually see. And there's something else. Their eyes are black. They no longer look quite human. He whimpers at the realization.

Oh, fuck.

And then there's the ones hiding behind masks and costumes. So many different versions of Jason Voorhees and Freddy Krueger. They all look so much more real than they should. Somewhere not too far away someone starts up a chainsaw. He can smell the smoke belching out of the gas-powered tool from where he stands. The person with the chainsaw is probably Leatherface. One of them anyway.

The sound of the revving chainsaw gets closer.

Suddenly no one here seems friendly anymore.

Someone pushes their way through the crowd of people encircling him. Mike sees bodies being roughly jostled out of the way. Then the girl in the witch hat emerges into the open area around him.

She smiles.

In her hand is a machete streaked with blood.

"Hi, Mike. Told you I'd see you again. Oh, this is the part where you run for your fucking life."

As if cued by this statement, John Bonham launches into a familiar drum pattern. Shortly thereafter, Phil Lynott plays the opening guitar notes of Iron Maiden's "Run to the Hills."

The crowd edges in closer.

Mike drops his cup of beer and runs.

THIRTEEN

SO FAR THE LONG-HAIRED stranger has only referenced the event responsible for the current situation in vague and ambiguous ways, but the bottom line is clear. Something bad happened to Dennis and his friends tonight. He's slammed beers with Dave and Steve for the last time. Those poor fucking bastards. He thought he'd be sipping brews with them when they were old men in rocking chairs. The blunt denial of this far-future vision is a bitter pill to swallow. Mike's fate is unclear, but hope seems slim. The same seems true for him as well.

"If I win this race, do I get to live?"

The stranger shrugs. "Like I said, I can improve your odds. I've got a lot of power, but I'm not God. Not quite. Without my help, though, you *will* die, and probably soon. But if I *do* help, I'd put your chances of surviving at somewhere north of 50/50. Maybe more like 60/40."

Dennis nods. "It's better than no chance at all."

The stranger grins. "That's the spirit! You ready to do this thing?"

Dennis grunts. "It's not like I've got a real choice here, but sure, let's get the fuck on with it."

"Excellent." The stranger tosses away his can of Lowenbrau and turns away from him, approaching the Z28. He opens the driver side door and stands behind it, glancing back at Dennis. "Nora's riding with you, by the way. She'll navigate."

He slides in and slams the door shut.

Seconds later, the engine roars to life.

Nora hops off the Z's hood and grabs the case of Lowenbrau in the last moment before the stranger puts the car in reverse and hits the gas. The Z shoots backward, its tires squealing as the stranger gives the steering wheel a hard crank, causing the car's back end to turn toward the store. The stranger then immediately changes gears and hits the gas again, this time streaking across the parking lot to the exit. The tires squeal again as the car turns sharply to the left and speeds away, its red taillights disappearing within moments.

Dennis looks at Nora. "I guess you know where he's going."

Nora rolls her eyes. "Duh." She jerks her head toward his Camaro. "Get in the car, bitch."

Dennis is slightly taken aback. He's never had a girl call him a bitch before. That the epithet sprang from the mouth of a chick as hot as Nora makes it strangely exciting. Given the grave nature of this situation, there should be no room in his head for lustful thoughts, but they're there anyway. It really isn't that mysterious, either. He's a young guy with a healthy libido. She's sexier than every girlfriend he's had since junior high put together. A simple equation, one he's certain she fully comprehends.

Not waiting for him to comply, she goes around to the passenger side, hauls the door open, and drops in with the case of beer cradled in her lap. She pulls the door shut, pokes her head out the open window, and yells at him. "Did you not fucking hear me? Get in the car."

Dennis gets in behind the wheel and jabs the key in the ignition.

As soon as the engine's started, he drives out to the edge of the parking lot and starts cranking the wheel to the left in preparation of a turn in that direction. Before he can do that, however, Nora leans over and grabs hold of the steering wheel, nailing him with a steely-eyed glare.

"No, jerk. Not that way." She hooks a thumb in the opposite direction. "*That* way."

Dennis frowns. "But—"

She sneers. "I know which way Lou went. We're not going that way. I've waited a long time for a chance like this and we're not gonna blow it. Turn right."

Dennis shakes his head. "I don't understand. He said if I don't race him, I'll die."

She scowls in impatience. "I know what he said, okay? I was standing right there and I'm not fucking deaf. But you can't trust a word he says and that's a fact."

"Are you saying if I win the race he won't honor his promise to help me?"

Nora laughs. "No, dipshit. I'm saying you *can't* win the race. I've seen this exact scenario play out more than half a dozen fucking times and it always ends the same way, with the challenger dead as a fucking doornail. Lou's car might look normal, but it really isn't. That black beast is virtually indestructible and faster than a jet plane. Now get your ass in gear and go the other way. You hesitate much longer, he'll get suspicious and come back for us."

Dennis sits there in thoughtful silence for a moment.

Then he says, "You keep calling him Lou. Is that short for Lucifer?"

She smirks. "What do you think?"

Dennis doesn't bother answering that.

He thinks things over another moment or two.

Then he steps on the accelerator and spins the wheel hard to the left, causing her hand to slide away from it. As he continues now in the direction taken by the Z28, she makes a sound of annoyance and settles back in her seat. "I should've figured you'd turn out to be just another gutless wimp. My seventh shot at escape and my seventh time being shot down. People say seven is a lucky number, but that's clearly a load of shit."

Dennis laughs. "You just finished telling me how unbelievably fast his car is. If that's right, escape is impossible anyway. Right? He'd catch up to us sooner or later, no matter what."

She sets the Lowenbrau carton in the footwell and takes out two cans of beer, passing one to him, which he accepts with only slight reluctance. "I've been trapped in this weird alternate dimension with him for three years. I think. Something like that, anyway. He's right about the way time is funny in here. This is a semi-regular thing he does. These races. And he has me ride with the challenger every time as a kind of test."

Dennis glances at her. "Like a loyalty test?"

She pops the tab on her beer and takes a swallow. "Yeah. And I've failed every fucking time."

"Does he get mad about that?"

She gives him a withering look, as if he's asked the dumbest question in the history of creation. Maybe he has. "Shit yeah, he gets mad."

"What happens?"

The withering look returns after a brief disappearance. "He showers me with diamonds and lollipops." The sarcasm in her voice is like the edge of a serrated knife, sharp and jagged. "I get punished, dummy. It goes on forever and it's always extremely painful. But he never kills me because I'm his favorite pet."

Dennis stops at the end of the street, holding his foot on the brake pedal as he pops open his own beer. He takes a sip and looks at Nora. "Which way?"

She leans toward him and puts a hand on his leg, adopting a softer, sultrier tone as she says, "Go back the other way and I'll suck your dick when we make it out of here."

Dennis sighs and leans the back of his head against the headrest. "Which way?"

Her mouth curls in disdain as she takes her hand away from his leg. "Go right. I'll tell you when to turn again." She laughs. "Or maybe I won't."

Dennis frowns at the edge of nastiness in her laughter. She could be teasing him, but he fears there's a good chance she's as untrustworthy as she claims Lou is. Ultimately, it doesn't matter. The odds are stacked against him whatever he does. He can only choose a path and hope for the best.

He takes the right turn and goes racing down a longer stretch of winding road.

"Is any of this real?"

Nora gives him a perplexed look. "You'll have to be more specific. Any of what?"

Dennis indicates the road ahead and the surrounding terrain with a general wave of his hand. "Any of all of this. The road. This car. The beer we're drinking. That strange store back there. How could my friends be dead already and still driving around with me until you fuckers showed up?"

Nora shrugs. "Oh. I get you. It's real and it's not real at the same time. It's confusing. This is his territory. Things get weird. He can, like . . ." She flips a hand about as if straining to think of the right word. "Manipulate. He can manipulate things. Distort reality. And . . . I dunno. That's about the best I can explain it."

Dennis nods. "Good enough. Do you really think you can escape, or was that you yanking my chain?"

She looks at him, all traces of mirth or disdain gone from her expression now. "He told me right from the start that there's a way out. Never gave me a clue where it is or how I might find it, just that I'd recognize it when I saw it. Whatever the fuck that means. I've been trapped in this distorted other reality all this time. Imagine that. You've only been here a few hours. Of course I want to find the way out. Lou is fun sometimes, but being stuck here forever would suck."

Dennis frowns.

If she's telling the truth about any of this, she must feel like she's trapped in a living hell.

He thinks about that a moment and almost laughs.

A living HELL.

Well, of course.

Maybe he *should* help her escape. Just stop right here or anywhere up ahead and turn around, go back the way they came, then drive around and see if they can find this mysterious exit. The effort will almost certainly be doomed to fail, but so what?

If she's right about Lou's car, he's doomed anyway.

He's still thinking about it as he takes the Camaro around another swooping bend in the road that turns into a steeply rising incline. Parked at the top of the hill and backlit by silvery moonlight is the black Z28. Lou is out of the car and standing next to it with his arms folded.

Waiting for them.

FOURTEEN

MIKE DROPS HIS CUP OF beer and runs right at the girl in the witch hat, taking her by surprise. He snatches the machete away from her with shocking ease and starts swinging it wildly about at the people crowding in around him. A lot of them are closer than he realized and more than once the sharp edge of the long blade nicks exposed flesh. The wounded yelp in pained surprise and start stumbling around in a desperate effort to avoid the deadly arc of the still-swinging blade. A few slip through gaps in the crowd and escape to relative safety. Others find themselves unable to retreat more than a few feet, blocked by the now much denser throng of humanity gathered in front of the flatbed trailer.

For an all-too-brief time no one attempts a direct assault. Everyone's still too wary of the flashing blade, which is now slick with freshly drawn blood. The last wound he inflicted was a bit more serious than the other shallow nicks, the blade slicing open one man's cheek when he got too close. That man's blood is still sliding along the edge of the upraised blade as another man comes charging straight at him.

This new assailant is a standard issue white trash hippie, a type common in the rural parts of the county. Always assuming of course that he's actually still in Rutherford County and not some weird alternate dimension, which isn't necessarily a safe assumption at this point. Shirtless and wearing raggedy blue jeans, his straw-colored hair is scraggly and long. He's got the red-rimmed eyes of someone who's been drinking and smoking weed all day long. The redness makes him look like some kind of hillbilly demon.

Stoned or not, he moves with surprising speed and doesn't stumble even once. Mike spends a full second frozen in shock. By the time he comes out of it, the only thing he can do is lower the blade and hope for the best. To his complete amazement, this strategy actually works, with the redneck hippie running straight into the tip of the blade, which punches through his flesh just above the belly button. His momentum is such that the blade goes all the way through his body.

By the time he realizes what's happened to him, it's too late to matter. He slumps toward Mike with his bloodshot eyes bulging open and blood gurgling from his mouth. He sets a hand weakly on Mike's shoulder and says, "Oh, shit."

And then his body goes slack.

Holy shit, Mike thinks. *I killed a dude.*

The girl in the witch hat shakes her fists at the sky and unleashes an ear-piercing scream of unholy anguish. It's answered by an unexpected boom of thunder in the cloudless sky. Tears spill down her cheeks in fast-flowing rivulets. Then she glares at Mike and comes running at him. He can only guess he's killed someone close to her. A brother or other relative. Maybe a boyfriend or just someone she fucks sometimes.

Mike spins away from her with the dead guy held up in front of him, the corpse still impaled on the blade. A human shield. He keeps spinning as she screeches and tries reaching around to grab him. She almost gets him when she abruptly stops and waits for him to keep spinning toward her. A hand goes toward his face and he feels long nails scratch bloody grooves in his cheek. He shrieks and yanks the machete free of the corpse.

This whole time the band has kept on playing that galloping Iron Maiden beat. The song ends as the long-haired corpse drops to the ground. A sound of rowdy cheering fills the void temporarily. At first Mike thinks this is the crowd expressing appreciation for the band's performance, but as the naked girl starts trying to claw his eyes out, the truth comes to him.

They're cheering her on.

A chant rises up.

Kill him! Kill him! Kill him!

Howling like an escaped asylum lunatic, the naked girl presses the attack. He shrieks as she gouges one of his eyes. He tries shaking her off by twirling away, but it doesn't work. She's clinging to him like a fucking leech. Realizing he still has a grip on the machete—albeit a loosening one, thanks to all the blood—he tightens his hand around the handle and starts hacking away at one of the girl's calves. She screams in agony and stops trying to blind him. Knowing there's no room for mercy in a situation as chaotically violent as this one, he pushes her away and swings at her again with the machete. This time the blade opens a thin red line across her throat. In those first moments, blood only weeps from the gash, but then it pours out in a sheet.

The girl stumbles weakly away from him, a hand clamped around her slender throat in a futile effort to stem the blood flow. In another few moments, she drops to her knees and then flops over to the ground, blood continuing to spurt between her splayed fingers.

She twitches and goes still.

Mike gapes in disbelief at the body of the girl he felt such lust for only a short while ago.

And he thinks, *Shit. That's two.*

There's a moment of relative silence.

Mike hears grumbling murmurs of discontent from the crowd. Somewhere out there that chainsaw is still buzzing. Once again, the sound is closer than it was the last time he heard it. *Much* closer.

The band starts playing again, another instantly familiar guitar progression. This time the song is "(Don't Fear) The Reaper" by Blue Oyster Cult. He has no doubt the surge of foreboding he feels upon first hearing those notes is an intentionally inflicted thing.

He looks around.

The circle of open space in which he stands has diminished. The crowd is edging closer. He sees murder in the black eyes of those not wearing masks. Action is required if he wants to survive longer than a few more seconds. Escape doesn't seem likely. There's too many of them. A whole field of adversaries. But he can't just stand here and wait to be overwhelmed. He has to fight. Or run. Or both. But where can he go?

There are only two options he can see.

He can try making it back to the woods.

Or he can run for the barn and try barricading himself in there.

But he can't decide and time is running out.

The sound of the chainsaw gets louder and louder. He's still turning slowly around, trying hard to keep a wary eye on all those around him all at once when he catches sight of the spinning chainsaw blade. It's bobbing up and down over the heads of people in the crowd.

It's maybe ten feet away.

Mike grimaces.

No more time for debate.

He raises the machete as he turns in the opposite direction.

Then he charges straight at the line of people in front of him, swinging the machete with the merciless vigor of a natural born slasher. The blade chops into the neck of a skinny guy wearing a cheap Jason mask. Another motherfucker who got his costume at

Spencer Gifts. Dark red blood leaps high into the air when he rips the blade free and immediately begins swinging it again. The blade chops into flesh again, this time removing some other guy's hand at the wrist. More red stuff jumps into the air. Mike shoves the handless guy out of the way and keeps on swinging and swinging. More people scream as the whirling blade tears their flesh open. At some point, most in the crowd appear to collectively decide it might be a stellar idea to get the fuck out of his way.

Mike starts to feel like the star of a horror movie. It's scary as hell but also kind of awesome in a really fucked-up way. He keeps swinging the blade and hacking at anyone still stupid enough to get in front of him, and soon he finds himself on an open patch of ground.

He now has a clear path to the barn.

The decision about which way to go has been made for him.

"(Don't Fear) The Reaper" is still playing as he starts running in that direction.

The ground begins to slope downward and he has to fight not to stumble and go rolling down the hill. He has a few close calls on the way down to level ground, but some desperate pinwheeling allows him to maintain his footing long enough to get there. By the time the ground levels out, the barn is no more than thirty feet straight in front of him. At this range, he can see it much more clearly. It's no longer a dark outline in the distance, but proximity only enhances the old structure's inherent creepiness. The barn is painted black. The main door stands partly open. Above it, the skull of a ram is bolted to the closed hayloft door. It's an ominous sight to behold, but by this point Mike feels more surprised than afraid. Given the overall aesthetic, someone should definitely have painted a red pentagram somewhere on the barn's exterior. The lack of one feels like a glaring oversight on someone's part.

He keeps running hard and soon is within ten feet of the cracked-open door. There's nothing visible through that crack but blackness. He doesn't relish the prospect of being locked in the dark in there, but he's all out of options.

Just before he reaches the door, he risks a backward glance and receives another huge surprise.

He's no longer being chased.

The crowd that became a mob is lined up at the top of the hill, staring down at him. They are no longer clearly delineated individuals. They've transformed into amorphous silhouettes with glowing eyes. It's a creepy sight, but Mike can't help laughing.

A few minutes ago their eyes turned black.

Now they glow.

That feeling of living inside of a horror movie comes over him again. And just like last time, there's a strange thrill underlying the fear he feels. Which of course is insane, but he can't deny that it's there. Instead of going on into the barn, he spends another minute studying the line of forms at the top of the hill. He still craves shelter, but he wants to understand why they've broken off pursuit.

He thinks there's two possibilities here.

Either they're afraid of the barn or something inside it.

Or he's been a sucker all along and they've successfully herded him in the direction they desired.

Not that it matters.

Either way, he's entering the barn.

A profound silence has descended over the land. His former pursuers make no discernible noise at all. No shouts, nor even murmurs. The chainsaw is no longer buzzing. The music has ended. There are no feedback noises from the makeshift stage. The perfect stillness is unnerving.

Sighing in resignation, Mike pulls the barn door open and goes inside.

FIFTEEN

THE TOP OF THE HILL comes up fast as Dennis jams the gas pedal to the floor for a few seconds. Nora turns toward him as he lets off the gas, an anxious expression on her face. The look is unlike anything he's seen from her so far, completely empty of her usual smirking attitude.

She leans close and hurriedly says, "In a second, he'll tell me to get out of the car. You'll never see me again after this. Please remember one thing. You can't beat the devil at his own game. It's not possible."

She turns away from him and leans back in her seat as the Camaro draws even with the Z28 at the top of the hill. The Z's engine is still running even though Lou is standing outside of the vehicle. Steam from its exhaust plumes in the chilly air.

Dennis brings the Camaro to a full stop.

He's troubled by Nora's words, her parting advice if what she told him is correct, which he doesn't doubt at this point. There's a part of him that wants to play chivalrous hero and go roaring off in the opposite direction before she can get out of the car, before Lou can even say anything to them. But he has only seconds to work with here and lacks the confidence to make a speedy decision under so much pressure.

Speeding off and making another attempt to elude the devil might well amount to killing himself, according to what Lou told him at the gas station. Winning this race is supposedly his only shot at saving himself. Except Nora says there's no way he can win. He's a rat in a maze, trapped with no way out, helpless to do anything but the bidding of a sinister puppet master.

Lou comes closer and leans down to peer in through the Camaro's open window. He's grinning when Dennis looks at him, displaying rows of decaying teeth set within blackened gums. "Took you fuckers a while to get here." He chuckles. "Tell the truth, Denny. She try to talk you into helping her escape?"

Not sure what to say, Dennis keeps his mouth shut.

Being in Lou's presence again would have him feeling jittery anyway, but the discomfort he experiences is worse than he anticipated. It doesn't help that Lou's face is so close to his own as he looks in at them. Every time he opens his mouth Dennis is assailed by his horrendous breath. It's an odor of putrefaction, as if he's rotting away on the inside. Maybe he is. Dennis flashes back to that moment when Lou and Nora were making out with such enthusiasm on the hood of the Z back at the gas station.

He wonders how she could do that without throwing up.

Lou laughs. "It's cool. No need to look so freaked out. It's what she always does. She probably even offered to fuck you. Am I right?"

Again, Dennis says nothing.

His hands are tight around the steering wheel. It's taking everything he has not to cringe and shrink away from that horrible breath. If this was anyone other than Lou, he'd be telling them to back the fuck away, but instead he grits his teeth and endures it, his skin crawling the whole time. He's glad Lou's eyes are hidden behind those black sunglasses. Their presence allows a small level of disconnection. He thinks if he could see those eyes right now he might piss his pants. Or say damn the consequences and go racing off into the dark just to get away from him for a while.

Lou tilts his head, looking at Nora. "Am I right, baby?"

She sighs. "You know you are. I'm sorry."

Lou shrugs. "No need to apologize. We both know the game here. Now get out of the car."

Nora complies without hesitation, turning away from Dennis and opening the door on her side without another word. She gets out and throws the door shut, her heels clicking on pavement as she heads over to the Z and gets in on the passenger side. Before she drops into the car, she throws one last look over at Dennis. In that moment, her features sharpen into harsh lines as her eyes shine with emotion she's trying hard to hold back.

Then she's gone.

Dennis feels a stab of remorse.

I should've done it, he thinks. *Should've tried to run away.*

But it's too late now.

Lou slaps the roof of the Camaro and moves back a step. "It's just about time for the main event, kiddo. Pull forward and get your ride turned around so we're facing the same direction."

He backs off another step, so that he's almost right up against the Z.

Dennis lets out a big breath and relaxes his grip on the wheel. His heart is pounding away like a jackhammer. He tells himself to calm down, but it's easier said than done. It's not every day you face off against the devil in a race to save your life.

He taps the gas pedal and the Camaro slowly rolls forward. When he's clear of the Z, he spins the wheel and turns around in a wide loop. Another goose of the gas pedal brings him rolling forward again. He stops when the front end of the Camaro is about dead even with the Z.

Lou comes closer again, but this time he doesn't lean down and put his face inches away from Dennis's own. There's that to be thankful for, if nothing else. "Okay, Denny, here's how this is gonna work. It's real simple, but pay attention. We're gonna drive straight for not quite ten miles. Well, not *straight* straight. This road curves like a motherfucker. But we're gonna go almost ten miles without turning. Keep an eye on your odometer. When you see the sign for Dead End Road, turn there and keep gunning it for another eight miles. Race is over when you reach the dead end. Easy, right?"

Dennis nods. "Yeah. Okay."

Lou turns away and gets in the Z.

For a moment, he's hidden behind that black-tinted window. Then the window slides down and Lou looks out at him. He puts an arm out the window and raises the forearm upright. "Wait for my signal. This is just practice, okay? Hold your horses while I demonstrate." He flips the forearm forward and revs the Z's engine. "Got it?"

Dennis nods again. "Yeah."

"One more thing." Lou turns away from him and appears to dig for something in the glove box. Doing this allows Dennis a brief glimpse of Nora in the shotgun seat. She's facing forward, her face impassive. Then Lou twists around again, blocking her from view. "This is more like a suggestion than a requirement. You can ignore it if you want. Play something loud and heavy to get the blood pumping. Some extra adrenaline might give you all the edge you need."

Lou holds up a cassette tape.

It's *Hell Bent for Leather* by Judas Priest.

"You want a minute to pick out something?"

Dennis is on the verge of declining the opportunity when he reconsiders. Loud music might make it harder to concentrate on driving. On the other hand, he believes what Nora told him about the race essentially being rigged. His loss and subsequent death are foregone conclusions. He might as well have some rock and roll blasting as he rides into oblivion. Mike's tape case is in the back, but he doesn't bother reaching for it. *Appetite For Destruction* is still in the tape player. He pops it out and tosses it in the back. It was the last thing he listened to with the guys. That's a closed circle. He wants something else. There are two tapes of his own in the glove box, *Kill 'Em All* by Metallica and *Machine Head* by Deep Purple.

As far as Dennis is concerned, the first song on *Machine Head* makes it the obvious and best choice. He grabs the tape and pops it in the player, hitting the rewind button to cue up "Highway Star."

The tape player clicks when it's finished rewinding the cassette. Dennis turns up the volume as the tape starts spooling forward. He looks at Lou and nods to signal his readiness, his grip on the steering wheel tightening.

Lou throws back his head and laughs when he hears the first strains of the Deep Purple song.

Then he looks at Dennis and gives him a thumbs-up, shouting to be heard above the music. *"Righteous tune-age, my man!"*

Dennis almost smiles.

Lou puts his arm out his window again and raises his forearm. His head turns toward his opponent and for a moment Dennis can almost see the red demon eyes burning behind the black sunglasses.

Then he flips his arm forward and the race begins.

SIXTEEN

ONCE THE BARN DOOR IS closed, Mike stands enveloped in perfect blackness for a short period. It lasts no more than ten seconds, if that long. During that time, his face is no more than a foot away from the door, but he can't see it. The door hasn't disappeared. He reaches out and touches it, feels the rough old wood against his fingers, but the absolute blackness conceals it. This perfect absence of all light lasts long enough to ignite a fresh feeling of panic, a feeling abruptly banished when the barn fills with light.

This is a strange development in its own right, but he does not immediately seek out the source of illumination. Instead he stands there holding his breath while he stares at the door, expecting it to start shaking at any moment as his pursuers begin banging their fists against it, but that doesn't happen. Another several seconds elapse as he stands there and awaits a delayed assault. Again, nothing happens, at which point he figures it's safe to assume the glowing-eyed freaks are still lined up at the top of the hill.

There's an old-fashioned latch mechanism attached to the door. He engages the latch and tests the door, deciding it won't easily be battered open, unless someone out there decides to smash through it with a truck. This seems unlikely, but Mike backs away from the door anyway. Unlike the barn's exterior, the inside isn't painted in that ominous black shade. What he can see of it in those early moments is unremarkable, looking much like the dusty interior of any crumbling old barn. He sees some tools turned brown with rust and a rotting barrel partially broken apart. Nothing overtly scary.

Then he turns around and gasps.

A large open area takes up most of the available space in the barn, and parked in the middle of this space is a recent-model Camaro painted a bright shade of red. Right away he knows this isn't any random Camaro. This one belongs to Dennis Ayers and he last saw it parked at the gas pump outside that creepy convenience store. Even if he didn't recognize the tag number, the Van Halen and Motley Crue logo stickers on the rear bumper would be confirmation enough. There's no doubt whatsoever. This is his friend's car.

But what's it doing in here?

And *how* did it get here?

To his surprise, he feels no excitement at seeing the car, nor does the sight of it fill him with any expectation of a happy reunion with his lost friends. What he feels instead is a queasy sense of dread. The Camaro's windows are dark, like the tinted windows of the Z28 that was harassing them earlier. This is strange, because his friend's car doesn't have tinted windows.

Mike closes his eyes and counts slowly to ten.

They flutter open again.

The Camaro is still there, which is disappointing. He'd hoped it was a hallucination, but of course that's not the case. On a night when bathroom walls disappear and mysterious paths appear in the woods, it's foolish to write any strange sight off as unreal. At the same time, he knows he can't fully trust anything his eyes show him. Reality has become uncomfortably fluid. He suspects what he perceives as reality may not be reality at all. It's an upsetting notion, one he wishes he could easily laugh off, but he can't.

Resigned to its presence, he decides he should give the car a closer examination, but before doing that he surveys the rest of the barn's interior. What he can see of it anyway. He thinks he's alone in here. It's possible someone's lurking out of sight in the hayloft at the back of the barn, but he doesn't think so. He hears nothing, senses no other presence. Not that he's suddenly psychic or anything, but he's convinced he'd feel it if someone else was here. As he looks around, he's also unable to identify the source of illumination. There are no hanging lamps or lanterns in the barn, no hole in the roof to let in moonlight.

The light is just there.

Defying explanation, like so many other things tonight.

Letting out a breath, Mike approaches the Camaro and touches the spoiler at the rear of the hatch. The car feels solid beneath the pads of his fingers. He runs his fingers along the side of the vehicle, feeling dust accumulate on his fingertips. Stopping as he arrives at the passenger-side window, he bends slightly at the waist and tries to look inside. At first he thinks there's nothing in there, but as his gaze lingers he realizes he's wrong. The inexplicable darkness of the windows made the forms inside almost impossible to discern initially, but now he sees them. Just dark outlines, but definitely there. Two in the front and one in the back. The backseat on this side is empty.

The reason that spot is empty hits him right away.

That's where I should be.

The forms are perfectly still.

Unmoving. Frozen.

Mike belatedly realizes his hands are shaking. His breath has quickened and his heart feels like it wants to leap into his throat. An audible whimper escapes his lips as he stands erect and takes some steps backward. His whole body trembles as he gapes at the car, a sense of profound horror engulfing him. There's something awful nagging at the outer edges of perception. Something he doesn't want to see, but it's trying to get in anyway, pushing harder now that he's aware of it on some dim level.

He's about to take some more backward steps when a voice speaks behind him. "The only way out is through. You have to get in the car."

Mike yelps and spins around.

"What the fuck? How did you get in here?"

The naked girl from the field is in the barn with him now. She should be dead, but here she is, resurrected like one of the Deadites in Sam Raimi's *Evil Dead* movies. The witch hat is atop her head again, albeit at a more crooked angle now. The horizontal slash across her throat—a wound he created with the machete still grasped in his right hand—has not disappeared. The wound has no apparent effect on her ability to speak intelligibly.

She ignores his question. "You have to get in the car."

He grunts. "Yeah. You said that already. *Why* do I have to get in the car?"

The tone of her voice is as neutral as that of a robot as she says, "Because if you don't get in the car, you'll stay in this place forever, never waking again. The only way out is through."

Tears spill from Mike's eyes.

He relinquishes his grip on the machete and it drops to the ground. The terrible thing nudging at the edges of perception pushes a little harder now. For a flashing second, he thinks he hears someone screaming.

He sniffles. "What happens if I get in the car?"

Her tone remains neutral as she says, "I don't know, but you will not be trapped in this place."

She blinks out of existence.

Mike wipes the tears from his eyes and turns around to face the car again. He has other questions he might've asked the girl, but he realizes that ultimately none of them matter. He's been told what he must do. Everything from this point forward is up to him.

He hears an echo of a scream again.

Faint, but real.

The temptation to stay here is strong. He could leave the barn and walk back out to the field. A strong intuition tells him the epic party would resume as it was before the divergence into horror movie mayhem. There's a band of dead legends out there playing an eternal concert. It might not be so bad, slamming beers and jamming to awesome tunes at the party that never, ever ends.

Mike smiles and shakes his head sadly, knowing he doesn't really want that.

Party over. Out of time.

The tears keep flowing as he goes to the Camaro again and grasps the passenger side door handle. There's a last moment of hesitation. Then he lifts the handle and begins to ease the door open, squinting against the almost blinding light spilling out of the car now. He pulls the door open wider and sees that the brilliant light now entirely fills the car.

Mike closes his eyes and steps into the light.

SEVENTEEN

AS HE HITS THE GAS, Dennis thinks about the last thing Nora told him before getting out of the car. *You can't beat the devil at his own game.* At this point, he has no reason to doubt anything she said. That being the case, he figures he's under no obligation whatsoever to play by the devil's rules. After all, honor is a meaningless concept in any contest against the so-called Father of Lies.

The Z28 zooms ahead of him even though—as far as Dennis could tell—they both jammed their accelerators to the floor in the same instant. Lou's car stays about a length and a half ahead rather than immediately pulling away to an even greater, impossible-to-overcome lead. He's either maintaining some temporary pretense at playing fair or simply toying with him. Or maybe it's a little bit of both. In any event, the immediate lead seems to confirm Nora's claims about the car's enhanced abilities.

He follows the Z down the steep hill and keeps the accelerator mashed to the floor to stay with Lou as he goes around the first of the road's swooping curves. There's a brief flash of the Z's taillights as the car goes around the curve. Dennis notes that Lou guided the Z into the middle of the road to reduce the severity of the angle and minimize the necessity of speed reduction. He mimics the maneuver without tapping his brake pedal, fighting the steering wheel to keep the Camaro from spinning off the road. It's a move he'd consider suicidal under any other circumstances, but he makes it without hesitation. Knowing he's probably dead anyway makes him fearless.

Ian Gillan's soaring voice rips through the Camaro's speakers, "Highway Star" turned up to the max.

Dennis sees the Z28 straight up ahead as he finishes going around the curve. This distance between the vehicles has been reduced to a single full car-length. Maybe even a bit less than that. This is definitely a result of his reckless disregard of the brake pedal. An unexpected giddiness infuses his emotions for a moment, but the feeling is tempered by the knowledge Lou is likely still toying with him. He's probably even looking at his rearview mirror and laughing at him, smirking at his desperate and pathetic efforts to stay close in the rigged race.

Dennis sneers.

Keep laughing, motherfucker. I'm comin' for ya.

They drive in a straight line for only about a quarter mile before the road begins to curve again. Dennis shifts in his seat, leg straining as he seeks to push the gas pedal even harder even though it already feels nailed to the floor. His hands tighten around the wheel as the road once again swings out in the familiar precipitous way.

Once again, the Z's taillights flash briefly as the car hits the apex of the curve.

Once again, Dennis doesn't even think about touching his brake.

The Z swerves slightly and the taillights flash again as Lou is forced to course correct. Probably too focused on the entertainment of his fucking rearview mirror. As all this occurs, the distance between them is first cut down to half a car length. Then again with the course correction. All the while, Dennis fights the wheel and resolutely maintains his reckless course.

He sees the opportunity he's hoped for as it arrives and he smiles.

The distance between the cars vanishes.

In that instant, Dennis cranks the wheel and angles the Camaro toward a corner of the Z28's rear bumper. His foot never leaves the accelerator as the Camaro slams into the Z, sending it into a wild spinning motion. The Camaro's wheels screech as it also threatens to spin out of control, but Dennis allows his car to drift all the way to the road's shoulder. He drives along the shoulder, still fighting for control as the Z goes flying off the road somewhere behind him. He hears a momentous crash of impact, but he doesn't look back and he doesn't slow down as he finally brings the Camaro back onto solid asphalt. The front end of the car is mangled from the crash, but the engine seems unaffected and that's all that matters.

He risks a glance at the rearview mirror and sees no signs of pursuit. A triumphant whoop rips out of his lungs and he bangs a fist against the steering wheel. It's an incredible moment and better than anything he realistically hoped for at the outset of this contest. He knows the race isn't won, knows the devil almost certainly has more tricks up his sleeve. In all likelihood, he's probably still doomed. But the glory of this one moment is real and he allows himself to revel in it while he can.

His head bobs as Ritchie Blackmore launches into the epic guitar solo from "Highway Star."

After gunning it down nearly a mile of more or less straight road, the beginning of another wide curve comes into view. Dennis briefly considers going around it in a marginally more safety-conscious way, but decides against it. He's not even quite halfway through the first stretch of the race. Sticking to what's worked so far seems the wise move now. This time, however, the curve is even sharper than he anticipated. The moment of recognition comes within an eyelash of being too late, and he almost loses control of the Camaro as he finally takes his foot off the gas pedal and tries his damnedest to work the brake and the steering wheel with enough precision to avert calamity. The car slides and drifts and for a moment he fears all is lost, but he manages to bring the Camaro back under control as the road straightens out again.

He glances at the rearview again.

Still no headlights behind him.

A check of the odometer tells him he's now traveled almost eight miles. The turn onto Dead End Road is coming up fast. He slowly pushes the gas pedal back down to the floor. His breathing quickens and his nerves turn even more jittery as his wheels continue to burn up asphalt with the road wide-open ahead of him. The prospect of actually reaching the finish line first still seems unreal, but a small part of him is starting to believe in the impossible.

As the turn onto the final stretch draws even closer, a grimace twists his face as he thinks of Nora. He wonders if he killed her by sending the Z hurtling into the woods. He hopes not, but if he did it's not really his fault. The devil put him in this position. The only hope of victory against a ruthless opponent is an even greater level of ruthlessness. He doesn't like it but knows he'd make the same choice all over again if he had to.

He takes the Camaro around yet another curve, a much gentler one than the last few, and shortly thereafter his headlights pick out the street sign reading DEAD END ROAD.

He slows and takes the turn.

"Maybe I'm a Leo," the second track from *Machine Head*, blares from the Camaro's speakers.

Race ends eight miles from here, he thinks. *I'm gonna win. Holy shit, I'm gonna win.*

The excitement he feels as this conviction comes over him is offset by intense trepidation over what comes next. This is no ordinary race. There'll be no smiling photo-op at the end. No trophy to hoist. No swimsuit model to pose with him in the pictures. And no fucking champagne.

A chance to survive, that's all.

And even that's not guaranteed.

A quarter of the way into the final stretch, the third song from side one of the Deep Purple tape starts playing, "Pictures of Home."

Pain *is* guaranteed.

He's certain of that.

He starts to go around another of those gentler bends in the road. As he does, he experiences a terrible flicker of awareness. For a second, the dark veil is almost pulled away. He sees himself in the car earlier with his pals, from before they arrived at the haunted gas station. When they were all still alive. *Really* alive. He sees himself driving fast around one of these sharp curves and relives that moment when the car left the ground for a second before he brought it back under control.

Except that's not what really happened.

The car left the ground, yes, but he never regained control. Not back there in his own world, aka the "real" world. Everything since then has only happened in this strange alternate place controlled by the devil.

His breath hitches, a sob trying to work its way out.

The final miles fly by.

When he reaches the end of the road, he's disappointed but unsurprised to see the Z28 already parked there, parallel against the dead end. Lou and Nora are leaning against the side of the vehicle with beers in hand. The devil lifts a hand in greeting as the Camaro rolls to a stop.

Bathed in the glow from his headlights, Dennis sees no sign of injuries to either of them. Lou's rotting flesh pallor aside, that is. The Z28 doesn't have a mark on it. None of this jives with the violent crashing sounds he heard after knocking the Z off the road, but he remembers what Lou said back at the gas station. This is his domain. His realm. The rules here aren't the same as the rules in the regular world.

Dennis sighs and cuts off his engine.

The door creaks as he opens it and gets out.

He doesn't bother closing it as he approaches his adversary.

Lou raises his can of Lowenbrau in a congratulatory toast. "Congrats, man. Most sincerely. You're the first to ever beat me. In this particular part of my domain, anyway."

Dennis frowns. "So I win? Even though you're here ahead of me somehow?"

Lou nods. "Of course. You didn't exactly play fair and square, but hell, neither did I." He laughs again and swigs Lowenbrau. "Truth is, you won my respect by being so goddamn cutthroat. You made the moves you needed to make and got out ahead of me. I never saw it coming. You win on the basis of sheer ballsiness alone."

Dennis grunts. "So what now?"

Lou drains the rest of his Lowenbrau and allows the can to fall to the ground after crushing it in his hand. "What happens is you reap your reward. You won the race and I'll do my best to make sure you survive what happens next. But first you need to get back in your car."

Getting back in the Camaro is an idea that upsets him on a primal level. His skin crawls at the thought. A part of him yearns to run off into the woods and see where else the wild night might lead him. It's a deeply odd feeling. He was just in the Camaro. Why should the notion of getting back in it now disturb him so intensely?

Lou's smile is almost sympathetic. "It's the only way out, bud. I mean, you *could* stay here and party with us forever, but do you really want that?"

Dennis shakes his head. "No, I don't guess I do." He glances at Nora. "And what about you?"

She meets his gaze for the first time and frowns. "What about me?"

"Was there ever really another way out? Or was that just part of the game you two play with all the unlucky motherfuckers who wander into this place?"

She sighs and looks at the ground. "It wasn't a game. You don't have to believe me, but I swear I didn't lie to you."

Lou chuckles. "Don't worry about Nora, champ. Her fate isn't tied up with yours. Her struggle is her own. The way out exists. Maybe she'll find it someday, before it's too late, and maybe she won't. But it's nothing further to do with you." His smile fades and his voice takes on a stern tone. "It's time to get back in the car."

Dennis nods.

An intense stab of pain in his abdomen almost causes him to double over. His knees buckle. The pain is bad, but he knows there's worse to come. So much worse.

He turns toward the Camaro.

Its interior is suffused with brilliant light.

He goes toward it.

EIGHTEEN

October 31, 2021

A STEEL-GRAY 2007 ACURA with an ungodly number of miles on it pulls to a slow stop at the edge of a quiet rural road. Michael Burnett cuts off the engine and looks out at the woods. At first he isn't sure if he's got the right spot. It's been so long since the last time he was out here. The last time was right before the turn of the century, back when everyone was worried about the Y2K bug bringing down all the world's computers.

Halloween of 1999.

Party over. Out of time.

Twelve years gone by at that point since that terrible night, but it was still too raw a wound. He got back in his then brand-new Lexus after less than a minute and drove away as fast as he could. That was when he was still doing okay for himself. Better health. Owner of two Blockbuster franchises. Plenty of money to spend on nice new things. A new wife and a promising future.

But all that fell apart and he never returned here again.

Until now.

He opens his door and slowly shifts about in his seat to swing his legs out of the car, getting out with a weary groan as his knees audibly creak. So many things are different now. He's around a hundred pounds heavier than he was on that night in 1987, for one thing. His marriage ended long ago and there's virtually no one left with whom he has any kind of close relationship. His life now is just an endlessly dull exercise in simply existing day-to-day. Anything resembling "fun" became an alien concept years and years ago.

Mike leaves the Acura's door open as he carefully steps down into the ditch. Taking a tumble is the last thing he wants, if only because getting back up again would be such a massive pain in the ass. He imagines having to crawl over to a tree and use it to haul himself off the fucking ground. It's a daunting enough image to make him consider heading back to the car. Calling off this fool's errand might be the best thing all around.

Instead he pushes on until he's out of the ditch and back on relatively level ground. He pushes through some brush and a few seconds later he finally sees it. This is the right spot, after all. Once upon a time the memorial cross was painted a bright shade of white and was easily visible from the road. Thirty-four years later the paint has faded and you have to get almost right up to the tree to see it. He huffs and puffs as he pushes through more brush to get even closer.

A lot of brown leaves are gathered at the base of the tree. He sweeps them aside with his shoe and sees some of the artifacts left there by mourners decades ago. A toy car that was probably put there by the mother of one of his dead friends. A metal picture frame with a faded photo. A baseball glove he thinks belonged to Dennis and what might be the remains of a stuffed animal. He also sees some empty beer cans that look quite old, including one of a brand that no longer exists.

On the tree itself are ancient carvings. They encircle the wide circumference of the old tree. Some were made too shallowly and are no longer legible. One that he can make out clearly simply says *Metal 4-ever!*

Mike smiles.

They were all so obsessed with music back then, them and all their other friends and acquaintances. It seemed so important, their identities so inextricably linked to the bands they listened to. The concerts they saw together were the most consequential events of their lives. Nothing else mattered nearly as much.

Mike hasn't been to a concert of any sort in a long time, can't remember the last time he could muster even the faintest enthusiasm for attending one. Music isn't life anymore. Popular music has moved in directions that hold little appeal for him. It's just something else in the background. Part of growing old. Eventually, the world always moves on, with all the things you once loved so much sliding inexorably into irrelevance and obscurity.

He circles the tree and reads more inscriptions.

There are multiple expressions of love from various people, each signed with initials. He thinks he recognizes one set of initials, most likely belonging to the girlfriend Steve Wade broke up with weeks before his death. Others might belong to family members.

Another inscription reads, *R.I.P. Dennis, rock on in heaven.*

Mike's eyes mist over as he feels the familiar old twinge in his gut.

You fucking asshole.

Dave Robinson and Steve died within minutes of impact, but Dennis survived. He walked out of the hospital in less than a week. Two weeks later, racked by guilt, he came out to this spot in a borrowed car, sat at the base of this tree, and shot himself in the head with his father's gun. He was found with an empty bottle of whiskey at his feet. Still languishing in a coma at the time, Mike had no idea until almost a month after it happened. Later he was told Dennis believed he'd never come out of the coma. He was also facing some pretty heavy legal charges connected to the crash. It was all too much.

Mike wipes his eyes and mutters a quiet apology to his friend. "I'm sorry. You're not really an asshole. I just miss you. I miss all you guys."

A sound somewhere behind him makes him gasp.

He turns around and scans the woods, searching for signs of anyone lurking behind trees. There's nothing. Nothing visible, anyway. What he heard was a quiet snicker. An unmistakably human sound. He spends a few more moments scanning the terrain, but there's no repetition of the sound. Nor does he see or hear anyone moving around.

He's about to turn around and head back to his car when he hears the same sound again. And then again. There's something subtly different in the timbre of the sound that last time. He realizes it's being made by more than one person. Then he hears a branch snap and catches a glimpse of furtive movement, someone dashing from behind one tree to another. A slender, fast-moving form. The laughter of the interlopers gets a little louder.

Mike's heart rate quickens as genuine fear sets in.

A voice speaks as he starts moving toward the road. "*Go on home, Mike. And don't come back until it's your natural time. We'll be waiting.*"

Mike quickens his pace through the foliage.

A third of a century has passed since he last heard that voice, but he recognizes it instantly, as if he last heard it yesterday.

The ghost of Dennis Ayers chuckles softly as Mike trudges through the ditch and nearly stumbles. He manages to right himself and press onward, not turning back again until he reaches the open door of the Acura. He doesn't see anything, but he hears a faint sound of music from somewhere out in the woods. He frowns as he listens intently, striving to identify what he's hearing.

Then it pops into his head.

"Reckless Life" by Guns N' Roses.

Mike laughs, his fear fading now.

Of course. How appropriate.

He waits there by the side of the road another minute longer, waiting to see if he'll hear the sound of laughing ghosts again.

But that doesn't happen.

Even the music fades away to nothing soon.

Mike wedges himself in behind the wheel of his shitty old car and drives away from this cursed spot for the last time, but he thinks he might yet be back again someday. In some other form. A lighter, freer one.

On his way back out to the highway, he takes a wrong turn and drives by a convenience store. He's almost gone past it when he slams on the brake and stops in the middle of the otherwise empty road. At first he thinks he's mistaken, that this can't possibly be the same place. Too many years have gone by. Memory is tricky. But the longer he stares at it, the more certain he becomes. This is the same store they stopped at that fateful night. Ownership has changed. The Union 76 sign is gone. But it's otherwise largely the same. He's surprised because for many years he's been convinced the store only existed in his mind, part of the landscape of bad dreams he languished in while lying comatose in the hospital for so many weeks.

But it's real.

No doubt about it.

He backs up and turns into the parking lot, pulling into a space near the entrance. The impulse to do this goes against his better judgment, but he can't help himself. He's too damn curious. Probably he wouldn't even consider doing this at night, but it's an unusually bright fall day in the middle of the afternoon. And unlike on that long ago night, there are other cars present, not one of which is a black Z28 with tinted windows.

The bell above the door chimes as he goes inside. The middle-aged lady behind the counter looks up from a magazine, glances blankly at him, and goes back to reading.

Mike takes a look around.

The layout of the place is as he remembers. Different displays, lots of newer products on offer, but otherwise mostly the same. His heart speeds up some as he walks slowly to the back, to where the bathroom is located. The door is closed. He tries the handle. When it doesn't budge, he experiences a small spike of fear, but then he realizes he hears a fan running. Someone's in there. He waits and in another couple minutes the door opens and an elderly gentleman wearing a Tennessee Titans hat emerges.

Mike waits for the man to shuffle out of the way before pushing the door open and taking a peek inside. He does it fast before he can think better of it. The size of the space is as he remembers it, but everything else is different. It's spotless, with all new fixtures and there's nary a drop of piss on the floor. It even smells sort of nice, the work of some kind of air purifier. The novelty condom dispenser is gone. He backs away without going all the way inside.

He's feeling surprisingly bold, but not *that* fucking bold.

A quick look around was all he needed to put some more old ghosts to rest. Or at least satisfy some of his curiosity. He starts heading to the front of the store when an impulse steers him back toward the beer coolers instead, where he grabs two tall cans of Bud. Years have passed since he last had any kind of alcoholic beverage. Relapsing now probably isn't the best idea ever. He knows that, but he kind of doesn't care and walks fast to the counter before he can change his mind.

At the counter, the clerk is ringing up another customer's purchases. While he waits, he checks out some of the impulse buy displays arrayed on and all around the counter. There's loads of stuff that wasn't available in 1987, unsurprisingly. The one thing that does surprise him is a display rack of music cassettes. He thought those things were long obsolete. Examining the titles, he finds a lot of country music and pop compilations that hold no interest for him, but then he sees one titled *Hair Metal Hits of the 80s*. He pulls that one out and smiles at the cover image of a scantily attired girl with big hair posing with a Flying V guitar. Flipping the tape over, he sees that a few of the songs are by those glossy poser bands he hated, but there's also several tracks he remembers liking back in those bygone days.

Fuck it.

When the customer in front of him moves out of the way, he sets the tape on the counter along with the cans of Bud. If he still had that latest new car he had to sell last year, buying the tape would be pointless. No tape player in that thing. But the old Acura he replaced it with *does* have one.

The clerk rings up his purchases.

She's kind of nice-looking. Maybe more than just "kind of." Only a few years younger than him at a guess, but better preserved. Some wrinkles and a bit of gray flecking her otherwise spiky black hair, but slender and exuding a natural sexiness a lot of women half her age would envy. There's a Motorhead logo tattooed on the back of her left hand. The name tag pinned to her shirt says NORA. He considers trying to flirt with her, something he hasn't attempted in years, but decides against it.

Nora gives him his total and he pays for his purchases.

As she hands over the plastic grocery bag, she smiles and says, "Have a nice day, Mike."

Mike's heart skips a beat.

He says nothing and rushes out of the store.

Once he's safely ensconced in his car, he rips the plastic wrapping off the tape and pops it in the cassette player, turning up the volume on Whitesnake's "Here I Go Again."

He pops the tab on one of the tall cans of beer and drives as fast as he can back out to the interstate, this time consulting the GPS app on his phone. As he speeds along, he thinks about the ghosts he encountered. He thinks about Nora and how she shouldn't know his name. Some spooky shit. But it's Halloween. Spookiness is in the air.

He looks at the blue sky and thinks again about how glad he is he didn't come out here at night.

Racing with the Devil soundtrack/playlist:

https://open.spotify.com/playlist/4rEZA5Rln3YKcNHp3xhr5N?si
=d0e5d499860949f7

BIO

Bryan Smith is the author of numerous novels and novellas, including *68 Kill, The Unseen, Slowly We Rot, Depraved,* and *Kill For Satan!,* which won a Splatterpunk Award for best horror novella of 2018. He won a second Splatterpunk Award in 2020 for *Dirty Rotten Hippies and Other Stories.* He is also the co-author of *Suburban Gothic,* written with Brian Keene. *The Infinity Engine,* a splatter western, is forthcoming from Death's Head Press. A film version of *68 Kill,* directed by Trent Haaga and starring Matthew Gray Gubler from *Criminal Minds,* was released in 2017. He lives in TN. Hobbies include drinking beer and watching TV with his dogs Mac and Roxie.

Other Grindhouse Press Titles

Printed in Great Britain
by Amazon

86825605R00068